The Christmas Match

MAPLE GARDENS MATCHMAKERS
BOOK TWO

PHILLIPA NEFRI CLARK

The Christmas Match

Cover by Wynter Designs
Editing by Lia Huntington

The Christmas Match

Chapter One

Isaac Spencer watched the raven-haired beauty hurry by. She wore the staff uniform for Maple Gardens Assisted Care and smiled at one of the residents, stopping long enough to collect a cup. He recognized her from somewhere, but he couldn't recall her being on staff. She was petite, and her long, black, wavy hair made him think fairy tales could exist. He shook his head and dragged his attention back to his mother, finding her smiling like a crocodile.

"What?"

Millie glanced in the direction the young woman was going. "She's pretty. Nice, too. Always remembers everyone's favorite drinks and makes sure we get something extra special on our birthdays."

"Who?"

Her pointed stare was one he'd been privy to several times over the years. She tugged on his hand. "Her name is Olivia and she usually only works on weekdays. You must have seen her at least once or twice. She's single."

"*Mom.*" He expelled a breath. "How many times have I told you I'm not interested in dating anyone?"

She stared at him innocently. "Who said anything about dating her?"

He leaned back in his chair and crossed his ankle over his knee. "Let's not talk about me. Tell me how your week was. I'm sorry I couldn't come for bingo night. I'm dealing with a lot right now at work."

Millie smiled warmly and brushed him off. "Don't worry about it. There will be other game nights."

She gestured toward where his close friends Bart and Izzie were sitting together. Bart's uncle Lawrence lived here at Maple Gardens, thanks to debilitating health issues, leaving Bart to take over the reins of a vast property empire. Isaac had been shocked to be gifted Maple Gardens by Lawrence and was determined to live up to the elderly man's belief in him. And Izzie's mother Margaret was also a resident, much younger but here following a terrible accident a few years earlier.

"Speaking of dating . . . remember how I helped those two get together?"

"Here we go again," he murmured.

"Oh, hush." She whacked his upper arm with the back of her fingers. "Anyway, we could tell they were getting close and then we noticed they weren't visiting together anymore."

"What do you mean 'we?'"

Her face brightened. "Lily and Alice. We've tried to get Margaret to join our group, but she's more interested in spending time with Lawrence."

"This isn't your little matchmaking cartel, is it?"

She waved her hand dismissively. "Cartel, indeed. We're just a group of friends. Don't you worry about it." Millie clasped her hands in her lap. "Anyway, I had a nice little chat with Bartholomew and it was a good thing I did.

Otherwise, those two wouldn't have realized just how good they were together."

"You have told me this before." Isaac glanced over at Bart and Izzie once more. They sure appeared happy. They sat together, holding hands, their heads tilted together as they spoke. Isaac's chest tightened. Bart had been Isaac's wingman many times. Neither of them had been interested in relationships—until Bart had met Izzie. But Isaac hadn't changed; between work and visiting his mother, he simply didn't have the time.

He didn't know what he would do if he had a girlfriend. She'd hate how little they'd see one another. Granted, there would be some perks to having someone he could come home to. But none of those perks were good enough reasons to tie himself to a relationship.

Isaac patted his mother's hand. "That's great, Mom. I'm glad you could help them. But maybe don't meddle so much." He glanced at his watch. "I'm sorry I have to cut this visit short. I have a meeting with an investor."

"Oh. I thought you'd stay longer." The smile dropped from her face as he kissed her forehead.

"I'll come back and visit again next week. And Christmas isn't too far away so I'll find some time to visit more frequently."

"Sure, dear. That would be lovely." Her voice no longer held the bright tone, and guilt swirled in his chest.

His mother understood how important his job was. And it was her long friendship with Lawrence which probably had something to do with Isaac now owning Maple Gardens. She had so many opportunities to stay busy and enjoy her hobbies—even if those hobbies meant she was more interested in matching unsuspecting couples.

Isaac pulled his phone out of his pocket, his eyes glued

to the screen as he headed toward the exit. The investor he needed to meet with today was in town for this week only and Isaac couldn't be late to this meeting. So much rode on it.

He swiped through his phone for his driver's number and collided with someone. A splash of icy cold liquid washed down the front of his shirt. Isaac let out a yelp, his arms coming out at his sides as he looked down with dismay at his ruined suit.

His eyes lifted, and he glowered at none other than that woman with the dark hair. From her nose down, she looked shocked—even a little apologetic. But it was her eyes that betrayed her. She was amused. Had she done this on purpose?

Isaac gestured to his clothes. "Look what you did!"

"I'm terribly sorry, sir."

"You should be. You should pay better attention. What if you had run into one of the residents?"

"Oh, I *was* paying attention, and it wasn't to my phone." She placed one hand on her hip. "Perhaps it's *you* who should have watched where you're going."

His mouth opened, then closed and opened again. Isaac gestured once more to his shirt. "I have a very important meeting to get to. I can't go like this."

She lifted a shoulder. "You could borrow some scrubs if you'd like."

"You obviously don't know who I am." He threw his hands up as he stormed past her. He was almost certain she laughed. A memory itched at the back of his mind, like déjà vu. As much as he tried to grasp at that thread, he couldn't retrieve it. Irritation sparked and ignited, filling him from inside out.

If he was lucky, he'd have a spare shirt at the office. Otherwise, he'd be showing up at the meeting covered in . . . what was it? Iced coffee. He shoved his phone into his pocket and clenched his hands into fists as he charged from the building.

Isaac held in an unpleasant word as he slammed the cabinet door shut. He did not in fact have a spare shirt and Mr. Frederickson was due to arrive in the next five minutes.

All he could do was pray this guy was forgiving of his less than professional attire. Isaac slumped down into his office chair and scowled at the wall. That woman's face filled his thoughts. Why did she look so familiar? The question was beginning to be just as annoying as the soiled shirt itself.

His office door opened, and his secretary stepped inside, hugging a stack of folders. "Mr. Frederickson is here."

Isaac heaved a sigh. "Send him in."

She nodded and backed out of the door to make room for an older gentleman. Samuel Frederickson had white hair, and his face was creased with smile lines. He had a neatly trimmed white beard and mustache and a round belly. If he'd had a red suit, he'd pass for a dapper Santa.

He opened his arms and tilted his head to the side as he entered the room. "Mr. Spencer! It's a pleasure to finally meet you in person."

Isaac rose from his seat, offering a crooked smile and held out his hand. "The pleasure is mine, I assure you."

Mr. Frederickson took Isaac's hand in both of his and shook it energetically. Then his eyes dropped to Isaac's shirt, and he chuckled. "Looks like you had a minor mishap. Would I be correct in assuming you have children?"

Isaac chuckled, rubbing the back of his neck. It would be so easy to pretend that he had children. He could blame the spill on anything but his own mistakes. But he wouldn't. He shook his head and glanced at his shirt. "I had a run-in with a woman."

His visitor's laughter grew, and he raised his brows a few times. "Your wife then?"

Shaking his head again, he smiled. "No. I'm not married, sir."

That was the first time the man's smile didn't reach his eyes. "Oh. Well, you still have time. I remember when I met my wife. It was love at first sight. It's cliché, but if the line in that movie was ever true, it is for us." He winked at Isaac. "She completes me."

A sense of unease fell over Isaac. Why was Mr. Frederickson so interested in Isaac's personal life?

They took a seat across from one another and Isaac retrieved a file and pushed it across the desk toward the man. "As you will see in those reports, Maple Gardens is a very profitable company. The numbers speak for themselves and I personally guarantee, if you invest in my company, we'll be able to put one in every state within ten years."

Mr. Frederickson raised his brows as he accepted the folder. "Ten years, huh? That's five every year."

Isaac nodded. "Correct. Honestly, that number is a modest estimate. With the right backers, we could beat that projected schedule by a few years."

"I've already seen the numbers. That's not what drew my interest. It's the atmosphere. Maple Gardens isn't like some run-of-the-mill assisted living community. It's a place where their residents still live their full lives—even those struggling with multiple issues." Mr. Frederickson closed the folder and placed it back on the desk.

Isaac straightened. "Of course. Maple Gardens is the best. That is why I'm confident my mother is happy. I was just visiting with her today and—"

"Your mother lives at Maple Gardens?"

"She loves it there. I make sure to personally oversee any changes and improvements so that they benefit the residents first and foremost. I have an excellent management team there and anything important goes through me."

Mr. Frederickson's brows furrowed. "That doesn't seem to leave much time for a personal life. How does your mother feel about that?"

Isaac pulled at his collar. Here came the personal questions again. "My mother is very supportive. She knows my work is important to me."

"Am I correct to assume you don't have a fiancée?"

"That is correct."

"That's a shame."

"Pardon?" Isaac chuckled nervously. "My apologies, but why would that sort of thing matter when we're discussing business?"

Mr. Frederickson rose from his seat and held out his hand toward Isaac. "I'm sorry, Mr. Spencer. But I don't think I can invest in a company that is led by a man without a family."

Isaac shot out of his seat and sputtered, "*What?*"

The older man gave him an empathetic look. "I'm a family man. I raised six children and I have fifteen grandchildren. They are so very important to me and I think about them each time I make a decision regarding my business and my future."

That notion was completely ridiculous. This was a corporation. The man needed to think about the numbers, not whether the CEO was *married*.

"Maple Gardens seems like a wonderful place, but if it's not overseen by someone who values the residents and their families more than the money, then it will inevitably fail."

A lump formed in Isaac's throat as Mr. Fredrickson headed for the door. Isaac bounded around his desk and held the door open for his visitor. "With all due respect, Maple Gardens is the most important thing to me—along with my mother. *She's* my family. I would never let it fail."

Mr. Frederickson stopped and patted Isaac on the shoulder. "I can tell. And one day you will wake up with nothing but a pile of money. What about your legacy?"

"Maple Gardens will be my legacy."

The old man chuckled and shook his head. "You misunderstand. Once you're gone, Maple Gardens will go on to the next CEO and the next one after that. Who will remember you when you're gone?"

His words had an unsettling effect. It was a good point. But that didn't mean Isaac had to agree. On the other hand, he truly believed in sharing the happiness his mother had found with the rest of the world.

Mr. Frederickson patted his shoulder once more. "Thank you for the meeting, son. Give me a call if anything changes."

"I have a girlfriend." Heat crawled up his neck. Why did he just say that? He never lied to investors. The numbers always won the conversation. Hopefully, he wouldn't have to have proof.

Frederickson's face broke into a wide smile. "Oh, why didn't you say so? How serious is it?"

Isaac shifted, putting all his weight from one foot to the other. "We've been dating for only a few months, but she's very special. Maybe by this time next year . . ." What? He couldn't tell an investor he would be married in a year. What would he say at next year's meetings?

The man winked. "You never know. Could happen sooner than you think." He glanced at his watch, then down the hall toward the elevators. "Tell you what, I have a Christmas party the first week of December. I'll send out my private jet and you bring your girlfriend. Of course, we won't talk business at the party, but afterward, we can hash out the details and sign a few contracts."

Relief washed over Isaac. He nodded and accepted Fred-erickson's extended hand. "Of course, sir. That sounds wonderful."

"I can't wait to meet the lucky lady. If she's as charming as you, I know I'll like her. Have your secretary send me a copy of that report you showed me."

"I will."

"Have a good evening, Mr. Spencer."

"You too." Isaac watched the man make his way toward the elevator and the second he disappeared behind those sliding metal doors, he jumped in the air and let out a whoop. His heart beat erratically. He was on an absolute high.

But then it all came crashing down around him.

Isaac let out a cuss word and charged toward his office. What was he going to do about finding a girlfriend? He couldn't find a real one. Convincing a sane woman to travel to New York with him for a business trip would be next to impossible.

No. He'd have to find a woman who would be willing to play a part—to be in love with him and possibly make a few additional cameos in the future if Mr. Frederickson ever made a visit to Georgia again. But where would he be able to find someone he could trust to do any of that?

Chapter Two

Olivia hummed to herself as she sorted files at the central station. As an administrative assistant she shared the space with the shift supervisor, another assistant, and any of the aides or nurses who needed to access patient information. A large, wraparound counter overlooked the huge common space and was easily accessed by residents and visitors. From here she could keep an eye on the needs of anyone using the common room. She loved the residents and wouldn't swap this job for anything.

Even though she'd had to clean up the puddle of iced coffee earlier, the look on the face of that annoying, pompous man had made it worthwhile. And although she'd shocked herself at the time, she'd reminded herself karma was involved. It wasn't as if their paths would cross again. She'd managed to avoid him on his visits with his mother and would continue to do so.

She stopped sorting and frowned. What if Millie found out?

You didn't think it through at all.

Olivia would never do anything to upset Millie. Or any of the wonderful people who lived here.

"You *should* frown!"

How long had Izzie been standing there? Her friend had the oddest expression . . . kind of halfway between outrage and laughter.

"I saw what happened," Izzie said, folding her arms.

Oops. She'd forgotten that painful man was friends with Bart. And Izzie was engaged to Bart.

"Nothing happened."

"*Olivia!*"

"*What?*" Olivia returned with a similar exaggerated tone. She glanced up at Izzie as she stuffed a file into the cabinet, then turned and shut it with her hip. "I told you ages ago he had it coming."

"You never said that."

Olivia's brows creased. "Don't you remember? He's the guy who dumped his latte all over me in the coffee shop a while back and then didn't even apologize."

"Yes, I remember you being upset because it made you late for work—but, Olivia, you never said it was Isaac who ran into you."

"Of course I did. I think I did. Millie's son. Anyway, it just kinda happened and I'm not sorry."

"You did say you didn't like Isaac. I thought it was because he was technically your employer."

Olivia froze. "Wait, *what?*" She whirled around, her eyes wide and her pulse quickening. "No. He's not my boss. He's a client. Well, his mother is. I've only seen him a few times." Her breaths shortened and a string of spiraling thoughts dragged her from the happy place she'd been in when she'd poured her drink down the front of that annoying man.

"Why do you think he's my boss? Isn't Bart in charge of this place?"

"Bart took over Lawrence's corporation—all those casinos, plus lots of other properties, but somebody else was gifted Maple Gardens."

"Somebody else . . . oh no."

How did you not know?" The corners of Izzie's lips twitched and Olivia scowled.

"Don't you dare laugh. I've never met any of the board or the owner apart from thinking Bart was heavily involved. I deal with Mr. Charles, nobody higher."

Izzie snorted.

"Izzie! I mean it. There's no way that guy is my employer. I think I would have recognized him . . ." Then again, how often was it that board members for large companies paid visits to places like this? It wasn't like she was some kind of manager. She had never had the opportunity to meet with anyone higher up.

Oh bother. This wasn't good. Olivia dragged a hand down her heated face. What was she going to do?

"Well, you threw a drink on the man who is not only CEO of Bart's holdings, but who owns the very carpet you are standing on." Izzie snickered. "Why did you feel the need to do it in the first place? You are better than that, Liv."

Olivia bit down on her lower lip, and the warmth in her face intensified. "What am I going to do?"

"I have no idea. I guess I could ask Bart to explain to Isaac . . ."

"That what? I held a grudge for several months and then threw my coffee at him to get even? He's going to have me fired! I don't want to lose my job." The tightness in her chest knotted up even more. There was no good explanation. This Isaac guy didn't seem like the type to let go of something like this.

"Don't stress about it yet." Izzie moved closer, her words pulling Olivia out of her own head. "I'm sure Bart can help. You're a good employee. You just had a moment of poor judgment."

"People get fired for less," she said dismally. "I guarantee Isaac isn't going to look past this moment of poor judgment. That shirt I ruined probably cost him more than I make in a week." She needed to relax. All these dark thoughts would only make the day at work that much worse. She forced a smile and shooed Izzie away. "Go enjoy your day with your mother. I'm going to get some more work done and try not to dwell on my inevitable firing."

"Olivia—"

"I'm fine. *Really.*" She gave her friend a pointed look, then flicked her fingers at her. While she would have loved to go get drinks and vent about Isaac and why he deserved to be doused in coffee, she couldn't. Olivia had never been the needy type. She was more than capable of taking care of herself. Izzie had enough to deal with between her new relationship and her mother's health issues. The last thing she needed was for Olivia to drag her down into a teetering state of unease.

She took a steadying breath. If she was going to be fired, he would have done something already. At least that's how he seemed. People in power suits loved wielding their control over others.

It didn't matter what kind of reassurance she attempted to give herself in her pep talk, Olivia couldn't squash the feeling that everything was going to come crashing down on her.

Olivia collapsed into her office chair, thumped her

elbows up on the desk, and she placed her head in her hands. She didn't know what would happen, but it was more than likely she'd be getting called into the manager's office any day now.

"Excuse me, dear."

Olivia's head popped up, and she met the bright blue eyes of Millie.

Olivia forced a smile and her hands dropped to the desk. "What can I do for you, Millie? Would you like me to set up a game of chess for you and find a partner to play?"

"That does sound nice, but not right now. What's the matter, Olivia? You look absolutely terrible."

Olivia bit back a humorless laugh. There was no way she'd tell this woman that she'd basically assaulted her son —and with iced coffee no less. "I'm fine. What can I do for you?"

Millie pressed her thin lips together in a tight line, then shook her head. "Nope. I don't believe that for one second. You have got to be the cheeriest person here. I can't remember a time when you weren't smiling. What's going on? You can tell me." Her weathered hands were clasped together and her stance was sure. She had no intention of letting this drop.

Olivia reached over the counter and grasped Millie's hands. "I'm having a tough day. But you know what? Everyone does. It's not what happened that matters. It's how I grow from it."

Millie's worried look morphed into a bright smile. "I like that outlook."

"So. Is there something I can do for you, or get you?" She released Millie's hand and picked up her water bottle to quench her dry throat.

Millie glanced toward the doors and then swung her

gaze toward Olivia. "I was wondering if you had found a boyfriend recently."

Olivia coughed on the cold fluid that was attempting to slide down her throat, which closed up and she sputtered, water flying from her mouth and her nose. She wiped her face with the back of her hand and let out a surprised laugh. "What?"

"A boyfriend. I've never seen you with anyone. I was curious if you're dating."

Olivia laughed. "No. I'm not currently seeing anyone. Why? Do you have someone in mind?" The second she asked, she knew she'd regret it. There was only one reason Millie would ask her such a question.

Before the woman could recommend her son, Olivia held up both hands. "But I'm not looking for anyone at the moment. I'm kind of a mess. In fact, I might not even have a job soon."

Confusion filled Millie's features, and she frowned. "Did something happen?"

Olivia shook her head. "I'm talking way too much. I'm supposed to be professional." She shot around the counter. "I'm sorry. I have to go get some air." She blew past Millie and all but ran toward the front entrance.

She didn't want to leave any of the friends she'd made at Maple Gardens. People would call her crazy if they knew, but this job was perfect for her. It was as close to a dream job as she could get. Had she just ruined everything?

Olivia darted through groups of people who were in the waiting area and when she got outside, she immediately buckled over, her hands on her knees as she sucked in one deep breath after another.

This wasn't a panic attack. This was something else.

Whatever it was, she didn't like it.

Dang it. The chances were pretty good that she'd have to apologize to the man if she wanted to keep her job. Not only that, but she'd probably be stuck with some of the more unfavorable tasks and schedules.

She pushed against her knees and rose to her full stature, then spun with the intent of heading to the gardens for a brisk walk, only to collide with something hard.

Olivia blinked rapidly and stumbled back a step as her gaze swept over the tall, firm body in front of her. His piercing blue eyes matched his mother's except for a fleck of brown in his left eye.

His brows were furrowed and the set of his jaw made it clear he wasn't thrilled about their second encounter for the day. Isaac folded his arms then glanced toward the building. "Just the person I needed to see."

This was it. He'd come back to fire her in person rather than calling her supervisor and making him do the dirty work.

Before he had a chance to speak, she held up her hands. "Can I say something?"

His eyes narrowed, but he didn't stop her. So that was a good sign, right?

She licked her lips and glanced away. Dang, his eyes made her feel uneasy. The lump lodged in her throat wasn't doing her squeaky voice any favors. "I want to apologize for spilling my coffee on you."

Still he didn't speak.

"I should have been watching where I was going."

Why wasn't he saying anything? Olivia lifted her focus to those unyielding eyes, feeling pinned against a wall even though there was plenty of space to go running off somewhere to hide. She twirled a stray strand of hair around her finger, irritation flickering to life in her chest. "Well, aren't you going to say something?"

Was it her imagination? Or did she see a hint of a smile at the corners of his full lips?

Yep. Definitely her imagination. Isaac Spencer was nothing if not incredibly disappointed. But whether it was due to bumping into her or having to hear her lame excuse for an apology, she couldn't tell.

"I have to visit with my mother for just a moment. Then I expect you to make yourself available for a meeting."

She swallowed hard and nodded, not trusting her voice.

Shoot. This is it.

Olivia had hoped to at least make it through the end of the week. She should have taken Izzie up on her offer to have Bart help. If Isaac and Bart were close, that might be her only shot.

Isaac headed through the front doors and Olivia shook her head, releasing a pent-up breath she'd been holding since she bumped into him. How was it possible that each time they interacted, they managed to crash into each other? If she weren't so terrified, she might have laughed.

Instead, her heart cowered in the back of her chest as if it could hide from the inevitable. Normally Olivia would have rolled with the punches. Had she been working anywhere else she would have easily quit before he could terminate her.

Maple Gardens was special. She knew it and so did every other employee. It was more than just the residents and the coworkers here. And she had zero desire to pick up and start somewhere new.

She'd never find a place as wonderful as Maple Gardens.

Chapter Three

Isaac didn't relish the idea of firing the young woman. But he ran a top-of-the-line facility. And Mr. Frederickson was expecting perfection. What would he have said if he'd seen Olivia douse him with her drink?

He could imagine so many outcomes, and not one of them ended well for the expansion Isaac had planned.

She has to go.

There was no other way around it. Sure, if it had been an accident, he might have been able to overlook her mistake. But he didn't get to where he was without knowing how to read people. Olivia had thrown her drink on him on purpose. For what reason, he still hadn't been able to decipher. But that didn't matter. She was a live wire, and he needed to secure his investment first and foremost.

Isaac moved through the crowd, straightening his back and peering over the people who hovered in the waiting area. The common room was just as busy, but that had a tendency of happening on the weekends. Most families had more time to visit their loved ones during that time.

His eyes rested on the familiar figure of his mother and

he charged forward. She spun around just as he arrived at her side, her face bright. "Isaac. I didn't think you'd be coming back today. I figured I'd have to wait until next week."

"That's sort of why I'm here. There's been a change of plans with my regularly scheduled visit. You remember the meeting I had scheduled today? Mr. Frederickson?"

She nodded. "How did it go?"

He fought the searing heat that crept up his neck. "Well, he's a big family man."

"That sounds wonderful. Didn't you say you wanted him to invest in a Maple Garden expansion? Seems to me you'd want someone who values family."

Isaac nodded. "Yes, but there's a problem." He hadn't planned on telling her this part. His mother would be furious with him over lying to get what he wanted when it came to anything, but especially business. A man was only as good as his word. So where did that leave him? "The thing is, I . . ."

It was the way she looked at him then that made him squirm just like he had as a child. She knew he was going to say something that would inevitably disappoint her, but she was giving him the opportunity to come clean first.

He sighed. "I told him I had a girlfriend."

Her expression didn't change. She didn't even look the least bit surprised. What was happening?

"Aren't you going to ask me why I would do something so ridiculous?"

"I expected you would tell me. Honestly, Isaac, if you were desperate enough that you made up a girlfriend, maybe you should get one."

"*What*?" That was not where he thought this conversation would go.

20

"Perhaps there's a small part of you that knows you should have been in a relationship before now."

He snorted. "That's about as silly as what I told Mr. Frederickson."

She shrugged. "*I'm* not the one who made up a fake relationship."

Isaac dragged a hand down his face. Maybe he needed to get his mother evaluated. It didn't feel normal for her to be acting so nonchalant about this.

"So, what are you going to do?"

"What do you mean?"

She leaned back in her seat and clasped her hands in her lap. "I expect that you have a plan for how you're going to fix this."

"Actually—"

Her eyes darted around the room. "What if you asked someone to pretend to be your girlfriend just for the week?"

"*Mom.*" Isaac couldn't believe what she'd just said. Was she actually suggesting that he continue perpetrating the lie he'd told his potential investor?

"*What?*" She waved her hand through the air and huffed. "There are worse things than telling a little fib like that. It's not like you're telling him a lie about the company. If that man is going to be picky over your relationship status, then you might as well do something to satisfy him." She let out a little laugh. "At least you didn't tell him you were engaged. *That* could have gotten messy."

"Do you even hear yourself right now? I don't know if you realize this, but I *don't have* a girlfriend. I don't even know anyone who would be willing to pretend—"

"What about Olivia?" She pointed a finger across the room toward the reception desk where the young woman who seemed to keep running into him leaned her shoulder against a tall filing cabinet as she spoke to one of her coworkers. She didn't look very happy. Her eyes swept through the room until they landed on him and the frown on her face deepened as she pushed away from the cabinet and pulled her chair out to take a seat.

He tugged at his collar. "Who? The blonde?" His gaze shifted to the other woman behind the desk.

Millie huffed. "No. Olivia. The one with black hair. She's nice. I'm sure she'd be willing to play the part."

Isaac frowned. "You're not serious."

"Why not? I really like her. She's funny and smart and pretty. I'm sure Mr. Frederickson would like her too."

"We've had a few—interactions. I don't think she likes me very much." There was no way he would tell her he had similar thoughts about her.

"Oh, pooh. You don't even know her. I'm the one who spends all my time here. She's a doll, and I think you two would get along really well if you would give her a chance."

His gaze landed on Olivia once more. Her profile. It was no surprise that she avoided looking directly at him. She'd probably figured out who he was . . . and that he could fire her with one conversation.

Unless.

He shoved the thought from his mind. If he pulled her aside and asked her to pretend to be his girlfriend under threat of firing, he could get sued, not to mention it being ethically wrong. But if she was willing to do him a favor to smooth the edges of their professional relationship, perhaps he could make it work. He'd offer to pay her for her time and make sure to get her the approved time off.

This might actually work.

Isaac would just have to figure out how to ask her without coming off as a complete creep.

He turned to his mother and leaned forward to press a kiss to the crown of her head. "I have an unrelated meeting with her. But I'll stop by to say goodbye before I leave."

She gave him a knowing smile.

"What?"

Millie puckered her lower lip and shook her head. "Nothing, dear. I didn't say a thing."

"No, but you were thinking it."

The way she could make her expression look completely innocent was a talent he had never mastered. "I have not the slightest idea what you're talking about."

He rolled his eyes as he strode toward the front desk. Olivia's eyes met his briefly before they darted to the paperwork she had in front of her. The blonde woman smiled warmly at him. "Mr. Spencer, how was your visit with your mother?"

"It was good, thanks for asking." He leaned his forearms on the reception counter and shifted his attention to Olivia. "Are you ready for that meeting?"

She flinched. He couldn't decide if he felt more guilty or pleased over that reaction. It was a good thing for people to fear him. Especially when it came to being the boss. But at the same time, if she was *this* reactive to him then his upcoming request might come off as something too threatening.

He stood and jerked his chin toward the hall where the conference rooms were. "Shall we?" He didn't wait for a response before he strode toward the room.

Cautious. That was what he needed to be. He'd tread carefully so she understood he was not holding her job hostage. Yes, he could have fired her for her actions earlier today. But he was willing to let it slide, especially if she agreed to be his fake girlfriend.

He pushed a hand through his hair, mussing it. Even in his head the plan sounded terrible. He should have never listened to his mother.

Scratch that; he should have never told Mr. Frederickson that he was in a relationship. He should have been honest about the whole thing from the beginning. But he was too deep into this now. There was no way Mr. Frederickson would agree to invest in this business if he found out that Isaac was willing to lie just to secure investment.

He sighed as he swiped the light switch up and strode into the empty room. His hands were clasped behind his back as he stared at the blank whiteboard. The room still had a fresh construction smell to it. People didn't use it as often as Isaac had thought they would. From the carpet to the paint on the wall, everything still felt new.

The door closed behind him but he didn't turn around. "Have a seat."

"Sir, I wanted to say—"

"Yes, you already made your apology." He frowned, his eyes shutting momentarily. Why did he feel like he was the caged animal in this situation? He couldn't just ask her to be his girlfriend. There was no way to make this sound normal. A part of him wished he'd pulled his mother into the room so she could smooth the edges of their conversation.

No. That would be even worse.

"I need to speak to you about something, and I need you to hear me out before you say anything." He turned around to find her wide, gray eyes on him. She appeared paler than usual. Dang it, she was more nervous than he'd expected. This was not the best time to ask this favor.

Then again, *was* there a good time? Probably not.

"I have a favor to ask of you."

"I'm really sorry, I should have just—" She blinked. "*What*?"

Isaac pulled in a deep breath and moved toward the long table. He pulled out a chair across from her and sat down. "A favor. It's a little unorthodox, but I want to make it perfectly clear that you will not be fired if you choose not to help me."

"Fired?" Her face flushed and she scowled at him. "I knew it. I knew that you were going to pull me in here to fire me. But you know what? Actually, I don't regret it. You're—"

"Olivia," he said firmly, "I said I am *not* going to fire you. I am up against a wall with an investor and I need some help. I figured after what you did today, you might be willing to make it up to me. But no, I won't fire you for your actions. At most, you deserve to be put on probation for such a display."

She clamped her mouth shut and her eyes narrowed. "What kind of favor?"

This was the hard part—the only thing he couldn't figure out how to phrase. "Like I said, I want you to hear me out before you make a decision."

"Just spit it out already."

He lifted a brow and her dark expression softened slightly as she slumped back in her seat. "Sorry," she murmured.

Isaac laced his fingers together and placed his hands on the table in front of him. He stared at them as if they suddenly had the powers of a crystal ball. Only they didn't. He just needed to bite the bullet and explain the mess he was in.

"I must preface this with one thing: you are under no obligation to help me."

She pressed her lips into a thin line. That small gesture was enough to tell him she didn't believe a word he said.

Trust issues. Great.

"There is an investor from New York who might be interested in expanding Maple Gardens to more states. Give more people the chance to live the way our residents do."

She lifted her brows but that was the only change to her expression.

"He's a big family man. And he throws an annual Christmas event at his home the first week of December."

Olivia's shoulders relaxed some and confusion flooded her expression. "I fail to see how I can help you with any of that."

Isaac pinched the bridge of his nose. "I was just getting to that."

"Well, hurry up. I'm on the clock."

He shot her a dark look. "You're kidding."

"I *am* on the clock." A smile tugged at her lips but he didn't find humor in any of this.

"I told him I have a girlfriend."

She sighed. "Look, Mr. Spencer. I don't really care about your personal life. Congrats on having a relationship with someone. I hope you treat her better than you treat the strangers you bump into at coffee shops."

"I was actually going to ask you—" He shook his head. "Wait, what? What are you talking about?"

A memory popped into his mind. He'd gone to get coffee after being up late the previous night talking to his mom. It was his father's birthday, the only day she ever showed any emotions about him leaving them both. Once she'd said a teary goodnight, he'd had little sleep and was like a zombie the next morning. He's lost the whole Americano Grande in a collision with someone on his way out of a cafe and been so tired he'd just walked out.

She twirled her hand in the air. "Just finish asking me what you're going to ask me so I can get back to my paperwork." It was almost like all it had taken was convincing her that she wasn't going to get fired to remedy her meek behavior. With how she was acting, he wouldn't have to worry about her feeling like he was strong-arming her into anything.

"I don't have a girlfriend."

Her expression froze into one of shock for a few seconds until she suddenly tossed her head back and laughed.

Chapter Four

"I fail to see why this is so funny."

Olivia wiped at a tear that escaped her right eye and laughed again. "Oh, but it is. This is what I call real karma." She shook her head and laughed again. This was too perfect. "You're in a pickle, aren't you?"

He glowered at her. But the look that was meant to make her shrink back in her seat didn't bother her anymore. Being told she wasn't getting fired had brought her confidence back tenfold and something about Mr. Isaac Spencer made her want to push back.

"So what are you going to do? This investor of yours—" Then she started connecting the dots. The investor had a party. Isaac had told the investor he was dating someone. He didn't have a girlfriend—and he needed one. She shot out of her seat and held up both of her hands. "No. Absolutely not."

He stood as well. "You didn't even hear what I was going to ask you."

"Oh, I'm not as dumb as you think. Seems to me you're in need of a girlfriend, and I'm a girl." She shook her head and let out a cynical laugh. "Did you honestly think that I would be the best option? I literally threw my drink on you." She clamped her mouth shut and her face filled with a searing heat.

Uh oh.

She'd finally admitted to dousing him on purpose. Now he really had cause to fire her. Olivia bit her lower lip. How was she supposed to back out of this one? She couldn't. That was the problem. Swallowing hard, she met his gaze. "I mean . . ."

"I figured it wasn't purely accidental," he said. "For the record, I don't think you are dumb."

"It's not what you think—"

"Look, I get it. You can't stand me. I don't really like you either. Don't you think that makes us the perfect pairing for something like this? Mr. Frederickson needs to see that I value family, and to him that means being in a relationship."

Olivia's face scrunched up into a frown. "That doesn't make any sense."

He lifted a shoulder. "I know. But sometimes you have to do things in business that don't make a lot of sense. Pleasing a client, for example, who has an old-fashioned sense of what makes a person a good man." He seemed to spit the last few words from his mouth like he could literally taste the bitterness of them. "It's only for a week. At the end of that week, he and I will have a meeting to discuss his part of the investment, and you and I can part ways."

This was all too much. She would have to plan a trip with a stranger to meet other strangers. Not only that, but she'd be expected to act as if she liked the guy. She shook her head. "I don't think I can do it. I'm sorry."

He pressed his lips together in a tight line. "I'm fully

prepared to compensate you for your time. I'm well aware of what you get paid here. I can offer to triple it for the week —plus overtime."

Her heart tightened in her chest. The holidays were coming up and she had used her meager savings on buying little gifts for all the residents that she was closest to. The cost of gas had skyrocketed and there was no chance she could afford to visit her family for the holidays. Her landlady had sent a notice about a planned increase. She would never tell anyone she was struggling. She didn't know where she was going to get the money for any of it.

Isaac was good for it. And he appeared desperate. He might be willing to do more than just increase her pay for a week. "No. I want a raise."

He arched a brow. "This isn't a negotiation."

"Isn't it? The way I see it, you need a girlfriend who can not only keep your secret but play a part that is convincing enough that your investor will believe that we've been together for years."

"And you think you're worth a raise? I don't believe this."

All it took was switching something off in her brain. She could pretend this wasn't the jerk who'd spilled his coffee on her all that time ago. He wasn't the guy she'd finally been able to get revenge on. He was a sexy, smart, and competent man. Olivia moved closer to him, slowly, sensually. Her touch dragged against the lacquered mahogany table as she rounded the corner and faced him. Olivia's fingers walked up his chest until she reached his hair. Tracing the area just above his temple, she brushed aside some of his hair and let out a soft exhale.

"I've missed you." She pushed out her lower lip into a small pout. "You work too much. It's about time you take me out on a real date." She lifted her eyes to meet his and something in her stomach leaped out of control as his blue eyes drilled into hers.

Olivia's mouth and throat went dry and she attempted to swallow back the discomfort. "You have no idea what I can and can't do. I'm very good with people. I guarantee I'm worth every penny. I assume there will be eyes on us at this party. How many women do you think would do this?" She stood up on her toes and brushed a gentle kiss against his lips as she shoved her hand into his hair and around the back of his head. It was a short kiss, but the spark of electricity that shot threw her caused her to pull back suddenly and stare at him.

He cleared his throat, his hand shooting up to gently pull her hand away from the back of his head. He lowered it to her side but didn't release her right away.

She could feel the blush returning. It had been a bold move. And if she wasn't careful, she could be charged with harassment at work.

Why did she have to be so impulsive? She didn't even really want this gig. But the pay raise would solve a lot of the problems she faced. Another apology was on the tip of her tongue but she held it in. If he didn't realize there would be a certain expectation for a fake relationship, even if it was short-lived, he was fooling himself. He needed to be prepared for all of it.

"Well?" She tugged her arm away; his warm touch was getting to her.

"Fine."

Her stomach dropped to her knees. "Really? You're going to give me the raise?"

He held up one hand. "Not so fast on that part. There

will have to be an evaluation to see if it's something you've earned."

"But—"

"There are legal issues that could arise from something like that. I will have to see if there is a position that warrants the raise and make sure it doesn't bring up any red flags."

"I've been working here for ages without one incident."

He gave her a pointed look.

"Okay. *One* incident." She attempted to hold back a smile but was unsuccessful. "But seriously, I have a great track record with my coworkers and with the residents. I'm well educated and often take on extra jobs without asking for more money. I deserve—"

"I'll look into it." His voice was firm and it sent a wave of chills down her spine.

She nodded. "Thanks."

"As for this favor—I'll need your personal information so we can get everything planned out for the trip. You'll need to pack warm. It's a lot colder in New York than it is here."

Olivia nearly rolled her eyes. She was well aware that Georgia had mild winters. Her eyes brightened. "Is there snow on the ground, then?"

"I would imagine so."

"And will we get to go ice skating outside?"

He gave her a funny look. "This is a business trip. We're not going sightseeing or—"

"I'll still get time off. You can't make me spend every waking moment with you."

"I suppose you have a point."

"And caroling. I want to do that in the snow. Even

better, can we help out at a soup kitchen or find kids needing toys or—"

"Olivia—"

Despite his tone, Isaac's eyes had softened.

"I know, I know. This is a business trip. But if this guy is everything you've said, I bet he would want to do all these things too. Maybe we can convince him—"

"I'm not sure what the expectations will be. I'll have to figure all of that out when we get there."

"But you'll make sure I get to do at least some of those things?"

"Yes. I'll make sure to schedule some personal time." He dragged a hand down his face and shook his head. "Please don't make me regret this."

She placed her hands on her hips. "The way I see it, you put yourself in this position. If you didn't want to regret this, you shouldn't have said . . ." She trailed off the second she glanced in his direction and found that dark look that made her legs go weak. She shot him a small smile then looked away. "I'm gonna . . . go. I still have some paperwork to fill out. I'm sure you'll be able to get my information so you can send me the itinerary."

"Yeah," he muttered.

Her steps were lighter as she strode from the conference room and toward the front desk. If someone had told her that she was going to get a job pretending to be her boss's girlfriend, she would have told them they'd officially gone crazy. Heck, she was probably the crazy one for agreeing to this arrangement. But if it meant a financial boost, then it would be worth it.

"What was that all about?" Cherie glanced up from her file. "I've never seen Isaac Spencer pull anyone but Mr. Charles into a meeting."

Olivia opened her mouth, ready to tell her workmate every scintillating detail of what had transpired, but then she snapped it shut. They hadn't discussed whether it was okay to say anything. And if she were a betting woman, she'd guess that there would soon be an NDA for her to put a pen to.

No, she'd have to play this right. If Mr. Frederickson was to believe that they were a couple, then, when he inevitably asked about her, they'd need a story. She nibbled her lower lip in a way she hoped made her look like she had just been bitten by the love bug, then she leaned closer to Cherie and whispered, "He asked me out."

Cherie dropped the pencil she was holding. "*What?*" she practically shrieked under her breath.

"*Shh!*" Olivia's head jerked toward the conference room where Isaac had just exited. Their eyes met and that strange bolt of electricity flowed between them. He was handsome. If he wasn't such a tool, she might have wanted this to be real.

But that wasn't how the real world worked. Isaac Spencer was as stuck up as they came and he was only good for one thing—helping her achieve what she needed to get her life in order. Manage her bills better. Not in debt to anyone. She gave him a small wave as he walked past, and flashed him a smile.

He waved back, but his expression remained grim.

Cherie's eyes darted from Isaac to Olivia and back before finally returning to Olivia. "Sure doesn't look like he asked you out. He almost looks upset. You didn't tell him yes, did you?"

"Why not? Is there something wrong with that?"

"He owns this place. If something goes sideways, then . . ." Cherie shrugged. "There's a reason all the television

34

shows do stories where the characters can't make it work. He's your boss. There's gotta be something against it in company policy."

Olivia sliced her hand through the air dismissively. "It's just a date or two. I'm not in the market for something serious. And I doubt Mr. Grumpy over there is either."

"Just—be careful. I mean, I like the guy and all, but I don't want to see you hurt."

Olivia gave Cherie a smile and patted her arm. "Aww. Thanks. But I'm sure we'll be just fine." She picked up her pen, then froze. There was no way she couldn't tell Izzie about this. Bart would hear about it from Isaac and if Izzie got her info from Bart rather than straight from the source, she'd be livid.

The second she got off work, Olivia would have to give her friend a head's up. There was only one problem. Should she tell her the truth?

Chapter Five

There. He'd done it. Isaac had followed his mother's advice and found a girl he could ask to be his fake girlfriend for a week. It hadn't been as bad as he'd thought. Olivia was surprisingly very good at reading the room and demanding what she was worth.

He almost admired her tenacity.

Almost.

What he did reluctantly admire was her enthusiasm to help those less fortunate. Such a rare and selfless trait these days.

A smile spread across his lips as he set to work composing an email for Mr. Frederickson. The first week of December was two weeks away. He had a lot of preparation to do before the trip. Ideally, he would have liked to get to know Olivia a little better, but they'd have to do that on the plane ride.

For now, he had documents to draw up. The man would want to see the statistics of operating the business here in Georgia and projected profits if a branch of Maple Gardens were to be opened in New York.

He had his secretary hard at work preparing documents for the trip itself. That meant getting copies of Olivia's ID for the plane's manifest, and putting together some basic information about himself, and he'd asked her to send Olivia a document asking the same. They needed to know at least a little bit about one another if they wanted to pull this off.

Though, with the way she'd been able to change her whole demeanor and kiss him in that conference room, he wasn't sure they would lean on it quite as much as he originally thought.

Man, that woman had the ability to steal his breath and all it had taken was staring into her eyes.

He shook his head to clear it and pulled away from his keyboard. Isaac got to his feet then strode toward the window to look down at the parking lot. The whole reason he'd considered his mother's suggestion was that he didn't like the woman. He couldn't afford any complications. And that was exactly what Olivia Todd could become if he let his guard down.

Luckily, she appeared to hate him more than he did her —something that only bothered him a tad.

He shoved his hands in his pockets and his focus blurred as his thoughts returned to the way it had felt to have her soft, warm lips graze his own. The faint memory of the tingling sensation she'd caused returned with a vengeance.

Isaac shoved those traitorous thoughts from his mind and dredged up the memory of her iced coffee against his skin. His hand went to the front of the shirt, half expecting it to be soaked through. The heat that had slowly built in his gut disappeared.

That woman might be a good actress, but she was still

just as hazardous as ever. He could see her being the type of woman who didn't mind digging her stiletto heels into a guy's back just because she liked to see him squirm.

He returned to his computer and resumed typing. One week. That was all it would take for him to get on Mr. Frederickson's good side. Olivia had something to lose, too, which would make them good partners. As much as he hated to admit it, she'd be a good fit—as long as she behaved according to their arrangement in front of Frederickson.

———

"What in the world is this?" Olivia held up the thick manila envelope Isaac had just given her. "You can't possibly expect me to read through all of this in a week. There's got to be over five hundred pages in this thing."

Isaac glanced over his shoulder. The cafe was buzzing with customers, blenders, and the coffee machine. Nobody would overhear them. "That *thing* is a dossier, and it contains information on me. You'd be wise to read as much of it as you can so we don't end up saying the wrong thing and getting caught in our lie."

"You mean you don't want to get caught in *your* lie."

He clenched his teeth. "Sure."

She lifted the folder with both hands, as if feeling its weight. "What about you? I don't see you holding a big stack of papers on me."

"It's back in my office."

She glanced down at what he carried and her eyes widened. "Is that the survey your secretary sent me?"

He nodded, then held out a smaller stack of papers with

little colorful tabs sticking out from the sides. "That is an NDA. I'm going to need you to sign it."

Olivia rolled her eyes. "I could have already told people and I didn't. Do you honestly think that—"

"It's not just about our fake relationship. It also covers subjects regarding Mr. Frederickson and the business."

"Oh," She glanced down at the document again. "Okay, I'll sign it. Anything else?"

He handed her one final file. "Here is all the information about the trip. Dates, times, and confirmation numbers. I've already cleared all of your time off with Mr. Charles."

Her gaze flitted up to meet his eyes. "Well, it looks like you've thought of everything."

"Yes, I have."

She huffed.

"What."

"Nothing."

His eyes narrowed. "You're going to have to actually pretend you like me, you know. That means no more eye-rolling, sarcasm or any of that." He gestured vaguely at her.

The corners of her mouth twitched. "Any of what?"

"The scoffs. Those little sounds of disgust. Mr. Frederickson will be able to tell that you despise me if you keep that sort of thing up."

Olivia started the process of another eye-roll then stopped herself. He almost expected her to stomp her foot.

"May I remind you that you're getting compensated for this? You don't have to do it if you don't want to."

She shook her head. "You're really clueless, you know that?"

"What is that supposed to mean?"

Olivia waved her hand through the air dismissively. "Nothing. I'll read and sign this, and I guess I'll be seeing you when I get to the airport. Do you want me to meet you at a certain gate?"

"That won't be necessary."

She frowned. "What do you mean? We're flying together aren't we?"

He shook his head, gathering his things to put them in his satchel. "I'll have my driver pick you up."

"You'll do no such thing."

He stilled and met her gaze, surprised to hear the sharpness in her tone. "Yes, I will. Beginning on that date, to anyone who might be paying attention, we are officially dating. Let me ask you something. If you heard I was dating someone and I let them drive themselves to the airport when we'd be taking the same private jet, would you think that was normal?"

"Sure."

He didn't know what to say to that. She was lying. Or messing with him.

Olivia continued. "Because you're self-centered." She glanced around the coffee shop and leaned forward. "And you don't care about people enough to make sure they are comfortable with what you want."

Her words shouldn't have hurt as much as they did. He was a businessman who, over the course of several years, had developed a thick skin. But when she'd put him down like that, it struck a chord. He couldn't let her see it. She'd use it against him if she found any weakness.

He clenched his jaw and pressed his lips tightly together as he stared at her through a narrowed gaze. "You will be picked up by my driver and you will show me and the company I represent the proper respect."

Olivia's eyes challenged him. She lowered her voice so only he could hear. "I'm not on the clock yet."

Isaac launched from his seat and stood, glowering down at her and hating himself for how much she affected him. "You are infuriating." He spun on his heel and strode from the coffee shop. The second he made it outside, the regret assaulted him.

It wasn't that he regretted their conversation or how he'd spoken to her. No, it was worse than that. He'd shown his cards. He couldn't remember the last time his poker face had failed him. Dang it, she'd managed to get under his skin and knew the exact buttons to push.

He didn't even know he had buttons.

His car drove up and before his driver could get out to open his door, he climbed inside. "Take me to Bart's casino."

"Yes, sir."

"You did *what*?" Bart's loud laughter made Isaac's head pound even worse than it had in the car.

"I know. It was stupid. But I can't back out now."

"Sure you can. Just tell him you broke up before you get there. The girlfriend doesn't exist. You could be all broken up about it. And no one is the wiser."

Isaac grimaced. "It's not as easy as that."

Bart sobered. "What did you do?"

A searing heat crawled up his neck and settled on his face. "I found someone to be my girlfriend."

"You didn't." Bart's shock was short-lived and he let out another bark of laughter. "Of course you did. I can't believe it. Isaac, who is she?"

"You can't tell Izzie."

Bart's eyes widened further and his mouth dropped

open. "No." He shook his head and got out of his seat. "You didn't. Please tell me you didn't get Olivia to be your girlfriend."

Isaac forced a sheepish smile and the unease spread further within him.

"You did! Seriously? How did you even get her to go along with it? She despises you."

"She threw her iced—" Isaac stiffened. "Wait, she despises me?" He knew she didn't care for him that much, but that was a strong way to put it.

Bart laughed again. "I bet you Izzie already knows anyway. I'm just a little hurt that they haven't told me yet. I'm usually included in stuff like this." He moved around his desk and leaned against it. "What are you going to do?"

"Well, I can't exactly take any of it back, now, can I?"

"No, I don't suppose you could." Bart stared at him with a contemplative expression, though the smile never left his face. "So how did you do it?"

Isaac shrugged and looked away. "I caught her in a precarious situation and asked her to make it up to me."

"You didn't do anything stupid, did you? I mean, besides the obvious."

Isaac shot a dark look at his friend. "What's that supposed to mean?"

"You know. Blackmail. Bribery."

He let out an unpleasant word and shot out of his seat. "Of course not. Who do you think I am?" Isaac paced the large office space. If Olivia despised him, she wasn't the only one. In a matter of a few days, he'd really messed things up. He stopped pacing and gazed at his friend. "You want to know the worst part?"

Bart gave him a blank look.

"She's terrible."

"That's not a very nice thing to say."

"It's the truth. She's rude, sarcastic, and she has this way of just—getting to me."

A sigh burst from Bart's chest and he pushed away from the desk. "You know what they say about that, right?"

"What who says about what?"

"There's a thin line between love and hate. Maybe she actually likes you but she's too scared to do anything about it."

"Shut up, Bart. I'm not going to let you get in my head. Olivia is a means to an end. She's the only person I could think of that would agree to this for her own benefit and then be willing to walk away without anyone getting hurt."

Bart smirked. "If you say so. For your sake, I hope you're right."

"I am right." He'd had enough of this conversation. Bart hadn't been any help, not that Isaac had any idea how Bart could improve the situation. "I won't see you again until I get back. If you need anything and I don't pick up, call my assistant."

"Enjoy your trip," Bart called. His annoying laughter followed Isaac down the hall and toward the elevator.

Chapter Six

Olivia rushed from her closet to her dresser and yanked out a couple pairs of socks. She shouldn't have waited until the last minute to pack her suitcase. If her dossier was correct, the driver would be here in about thirty minutes.

She'd struggled to get to sleep last night and then woken a few times. Worrying. Her head ached and her extremities were numb as if they weren't getting enough blood flow. There had been a list of things she needed to bring but she couldn't find it anywhere.

Somewhere in her mess of a room, her phone rang.

She tossed clothes aside as the persistent sound added to her increasingly irritating headache. Finally a flash of light caught her attention and she pulled the phone out from under a pair of pajama pants.

Without looking at the caller ID, she swiped to answer it, hugging the device between her ear and her shoulder. "Yeah."

"When were you going to tell me that you are going away for a week with Isaac Spencer!" Izzie's accusatory voice ripped through the phone and Olivia held it away from her head, grimacing as a sharp pain stabbed her behind the eyes.

When Izzie's voice was no longer blaring through the speaker, she brought the phone back to her ear. "I'm sorry, but I can't talk about that right now. I'm trying to get packed."

"Don't you dare hang up on me. You put me on speaker if you have to. What's going on? I can't believe I heard about this from Bart."

Bother. I should have told you.

She hadn't expected Isaac to say something to them.

She tapped the screen on her phone and put it on speaker, then put it down while she threw some more clothes into her suitcase. "I didn't tell you because I knew you would act like this."

"Act like what? Honestly, Liv. I'm not acting any different than a best friend ought to. Are you guys dating? Did you finally give him a chance? Wait! Have you been secretly dating behind my back?"

"What? No!" She groaned, rubbing her temples with her fingers. "Bart didn't give you details?"

"What details?" Izzie barked. "There are details?"

She let out a sigh. "He needed help with something— impressing a client, I think. And he asked me if I would help. You know I'm good with people."

Silence stretched between them and the seconds continued to tick by. She couldn't tell if Izzie was upset about this information, disappointed, or if she even believed a word Olivia had said.

Olivia shifted her weight from one foot to the other. "I swear, Izzie. Nothing is going on." If Bart hadn't mentioned any details about their agreement, she didn't even know if she could tell Izzie about her fake relationship status.

"So that's it then. You're going on a business trip with Isaac."

"That's it."

More silence. Then she clicked her tongue. "I don't buy it. There's something else going on and I'm going to find out."

"Izzie, please don't. He made me sign an NDA."

"You're joking, right?"

"No, I'm being perfectly serious. Until things are settled with the business side of things he wants to keep it quiet. I don't know much, but I know I'm not allowed to talk about it."

"Geez." Izzie's voice softened. "Are you okay with this? He better be paying you for it."

Olivia cringed. Isaac *had* agreed to monetary compensation, but it wasn't set in stone—so it was up in the air for now, however confident she was that her raise would be approved based on her merit. "Everything is on the up and up. Thanks for your concern, but everything is fine. I'll be back in a week and if everything works out, I'll tell you all about it."

"Are you sure? Because I can call Bart right now and—"

There was a knock on her door and Olivia jumped. Ten minutes early! She needed more time.

"Look, I gotta go. I'll call you later."

"But—"

Olivia tapped on the "end call" icon and hurried across the room. Her foot snagged on a power cord and she hopped a few times to prevent herself from colliding with the floor. "Who's there?"

"Isaac."

She froze, her hand on the doorknob as she peered through the spyhole. He stood stiff and all business-like out in her hallway. Then he glanced at his watch before lifting his focus to the door. "Are you going to let me in?"

Olivia fumbled with the doorknob and yanked the door open. The air from the motion blew strands of hair into her face and she brushed them aside. "You're early."

He looked at his watch again. "I'm not."

"Yes you are. My packet said the driver would be picking me up in ten minutes."

He glanced over her shoulder into her apartment and that judgmental frown filled his face. "Are you even ready?" He moved past her and strode inside.

She scrambled around and hurried after him. "I had ten more minutes, remember?" Her foot caught on that cord but this time she was too distracted to hop out of it. She shuffled, lost her balance and her body pitched forward.

One moment she was flying through the air—or at least that's what it felt like.

And in the next, she was being held up by a pair of strong arms.

Olivia craned her neck back to stare into Isaac's stern face. One look from him and she clambered to her feet. Her hands yanked at her shirt, even though it wasn't out of place. "Sorry."

"You're not ready and the plane leaves in forty-five minutes." Disdain dripped from his voice like oil oozing from a broken-down car.

"I *had* ten more minutes." She scowled at him and her hands moved to pull her hair into a messy bun. "If you had just waited—"

He turned around and let out a sigh. "There's no way you would have made this work in ten minutes." Isaac pulled out his phone and typed in a number. "It's Spencer. I need you to delay our flight. We'll be a little late."

Her eyes widened. "You didn't have to do that. I can still make it work."

Isaac hung up the phone and gestured around them. "Somehow I highly doubt that."

She sucked in a breath. "Well, you don't have to be so mean about it."

He gave her a blank stare. "My apologies for stating how it is."

Her face burned with indignation and she shoved past him. "Just you wait. I'm going to get us out of here in five." Without looking at what she was throwing into her suitcase, she gathered up an armful of clothes then dropped them on top. She tossed in her curling iron, her computer, and her chargers then added her slippers for good measure.

"You can't be serious," he groaned as he dragged a hand down his face.

She stepped back, eyeing the suitcase. "You're right. I'm wearing these on the plane." Olivia reached for the slippers then slammed the suitcase shut. "See? I'm ready."

Isaac pinched the bridge of his nose and let out another exaggerated sigh. "You can't wear slippers on a private jet."

"Why not? It's not like anyone is going to see me."

He gave her an incredulous look. "There's a dress code."

She placed her slippers on her feet and moved toward him, reveling in the way he stiffened at her closeness. Her fingers reached for his silk tie and she pretended to straighten it. "But who decides what the dress code is?"

Isaac worked his jaw. "If you think it's me, you're wrong. This plane is owned by the company."

She tapped his nose and walked back to her suitcase. "And you own the company."

"No, I don't. What gave you that idea?"

Olivia tugged her suitcase to the floor with a thud and rolled it toward the door. "You're the CEO, aren't you?"

"Yes, but that doesn't mean I own the company. There's a board and stockholders. Even Maple Gardens, which I do own, has a board."

She frowned. "Oh." Then she shrugged and the suitcase rolled over his shoe. "But as CEO, you can let me break dress code because I'm your girlfriend, right?" She couldn't help the feeling of immense pleasure she got from ruffling Isaac's feathers. He had no clue what he was getting himself into when he'd asked her along for this ride.

The thought occurred to her that she probably should feel bad, but that moment was fleeting.

Olivia pulled open the apartment door then glanced over her shoulder to where Isaac had remained. "I told you I was only going to be five minutes. Are you coming?"

He shook his head and trudged forward. "Are you sure you've got everything? New York is a lot colder—"

She rolled her eyes and placed her free hand on her hip. "I know that it's cold there. Just because I've grown up in Georgia doesn't mean I don't understand how the weather works." Olivia pulled her lower lip between her teeth and glanced away from him. She hadn't been checking when she'd dumped everything on her bed. But as long as she had her coat and a pair of pants, she should be fine.

Isaac reached for her suitcase as they got into the hall and his hand brushed hers. She yanked the luggage toward her, hating the way her heart fluttered ever so slightly. It wasn't the way he touched her. It was her instincts to protect her belongings that stirred that reaction.

Olivia's cheeks seared with heat. "I've got it, thank you."

He shook his head. "Out of the question. I'm sure you're

more than capable of carrying your luggage, but my mother raised me better than that. Please allow me to handle it for you."

She glanced from the case to Isaac and back. It was rather sweet of him to offer. The way he'd said it didn't make her feel like he was judging her or putting her down —a fact that almost surprised her.

Olivia nudged the suitcase forward and allowed him to take the handle, being careful not to allow his hand to brush against hers this time. Then she moved past him again, staying focused on not touching him. Her precautions might be silly, but until she could be sure she was staying in control of her emotions while she was around him, she couldn't be too careful.

The limo that waited for them outside wasn't quite what she was expecting. It was shorter than the stretch limos she always saw in the movies, but longer than a four-door sedan. The driver stood outside, straight and professional with his hands behind his back. When Isaac appeared, the man moved toward the door and held it open.

She didn't miss the way his gaze dipped to her bright red furry slippers and she grinned. "You like them? You can get a pair just like these at your local Target."

The corners of his mouth twitched but didn't pull into a full smile. Tough crowd. She dipped into the vehicle and waited for Isaac to join her. When he climbed in, the door was shut and they were off.

Isaac stared at her furry feet, the frown between his eyes deepening. "Please tell me you have a pair of shoes you can change into while we're on the plane."

She waved her hand dismissively through the air. "Relax. I'm not going to embarrass you. But I'm not going to change until we're closer to our destination. I refuse to travel in anything less than one hundred percent comfortable attire. That means my slippers are a must."

He shook his head, then stared out the window. She could practically see the cogs in his brain whirring. Isaac was just starting to regret his decision. It was in the way he kept glancing at her like she might grow horns or an extra head.

Olivia leaned back in her chair and flashed him a smile the next time he met her gaze. "You need to relax, buddy. This will be fun. It's a week of showing me off, and, despite what you might assume, I can be *very* charming."

"You mean it gets better than dumping iced coffee on me and insisting on wearing sleepwear on private jets? I can't wait."

She straightened. "I mean it. I'm a total catch. If I really wanted to, I could have been married off to some rich dude already. You're not all that special, you know."

That statement got a reaction. Isaac stiffened in his seat and folded his arms. His eyes swept over to her and then shifted toward the window once more.

"What? You don't believe me? Because—"

His intense gaze landed on her, cutting off the words that had once flown from her mouth so easily. "I believe that you are very attractive and you could have your pick of nearly anyone. But you're loud, messy, and inordinately infuriating."

She gasped. That was not what she'd expected him to say to her. Any possible retort had been doused by his statement. Her face flushed and she scowled. She'd show him. She'd be the perfect girlfriend—so perfect that he'd be begging her to date him for real and she could put him down hard just like he'd done to her.

Chapter Seven

Isaac needed to put a stop to the construction zone his chest had become. The incessant hammering of his heart was messing with the calming whirring of his thoughts. There was just something intoxicating about Olivia that had thrown him so far off balance that he couldn't think straight.

And he downright hated it.

She wasn't the kind of woman he would want to bring home. Everything he'd said was completely true. She wasn't marriage material so it was a darn good thing he wasn't interested in getting married. Even better that he hadn't told Mr. Frederickson that he was engaged.

Isaac peeked in Olivia's direction, surprised to find her sulking. The words he'd thrown at her hadn't been intentionally hurtful. But now that he went over them once more, he cringed. His mother would have put him in his place for saying such things to a girl who was willing to help get him out of the mess he'd put himself into.

He fidgeted in his seat, shooting more quick looks at her. When she wasn't talking or berating him, she was really rather beautiful. She had the largest steel-gray eyes he'd ever seen. Her nose turned up a little at the end and her lips were the perfect shade of rose pink. Her dark locks accentuated her features, making her look like a porcelain doll.

Isaac shook his head and shut his eyes to ward off the feelings that were already brewing within him. This wasn't good. He had to be objective. He wasn't on this trip to find a woman to date. He was here because he wanted to expand Maple Gardens to other parts of the country and give more people the chance to experience what he could offer.

If Olivia's presence was going to distract him, he was in trouble. Inwardly, he cursed himself for allowing her to get under his skin. She was no different from any other woman he might have found. She was just a placeholder while Mr. Frederickson decided to move forward with his investment.

And then we can go our separate ways.

The car pulled to a stop and they exited the car. He surged for the small office where they'd be going through their personal pre-flight security check. Their plane was prepped for their arrival several yards away. Olivia wasn't beside him when he reached the door and he turned around to find her arguing with the driver.

"It's my bag. I can take my own property to the airplane."

"I'm sorry, miss, but there are certain regulations in place. You can't—"

"This is a private jet. I'm allowed to bring my—"

Isaac bit back a smile and hurried toward her.

Olivia glanced at him as he approached then gestured toward the man. "Will you tell him that I can take my own darn luggage?"

He placed his hand on the small of her back, and

jumped as a spark of electricity ignited between them. That was strange, but she didn't seem to notice. So he gently turned her toward the building and murmured, "Have you ever flown on a private plane before?"

"No. Why?"

"Well, there are still rules and precautions. He'll take your luggage to the security checkpoint. Don't worry." The warmth of her body flowed into his hand as he continued moving with her toward the building.

She glanced over her shoulder for a moment, then her eyes lifted to meet his. "He better not lose it. I have everything in there."

"He's going to take mine too. It'll be fine."

They made it through security without much mishap, though Olivia still got some strange looks when people noticed her fuzzy slippers. Most of the travelers in the small building were dressed much like himself—business attire. Olivia was the only one who stood out, wearing a superhero t-shirt, tattered capris, and those blasted bright red slippers.

Once they made it through security, an attendant escorted them toward their plane. This time, Olivia stayed close, only there was one unexpected change. Her small, warm hand slipped into his own and she laced her fingers with his.

He stilled as his gaze dipped down to their interlocked hands. What was she trying to accomplish? Was she trying to butter him up? Because it wasn't going to work. Except even as the thought crossed his mind, a small smile stole across his face.

Each time they'd touched, the experience had been . . . pleasant.

Nope.

Shut it down, Spencer.

This line of thinking was dangerous. Not only for his own mental state, but because she was his employee. The lawsuits alone that could be filed if the thin gray line that had been drawn between them blurred gave him enough cause to pull his hand from her grasp.

Luckily they'd arrived at the stairs to the plane at that exact moment. Anyone who was paying attention wouldn't have thought a single thing of it. Isaac motioned for Olivia to take the lead and head up to the plane first. His phone rang and she paused to look at him.

Isaac nodded. "I'll be just a minute. Go ahead and pick a seat."

She hesitated, her eyes lifting toward the door of the plane.

Without waiting for her to get the confidence to oblige, Isaac answered the call and strode a few steps away.

"Spencer here."

"Ah, Mr. Spencer. I was hoping to catch you before your plane took off." Mr. Frederickson's voice drifted from the receiver. "I wanted to ask what your girlfriend's favorite meal is. My wife has this tradition of asking the chef to whip up something special for our guests."

Isaac whirled around just in time to see Olivia disappear inside the plane.

"Isaac? Are you still there?"

He cleared his throat. "Yes, I'm here. Honestly, neither one of us have specific tastes. You can have your chef prepare anything you'd like."

"Nonsense," Mr. Frederickson chuckled. "Lucille would have my head if she thought for one second I accepted that sort of statement. You and your lovely girlfriend will be our special guests for the week and we want to start it off right."

Isaac stole one more glance toward the plane. It wasn't like he could skip the steps and make his way up there in enough time to get the answer. He should know this. He had the survey his secretary had sent over. But he hadn't looked at it yet—he had planned on doing a crash course on her while the plane was in flight.

What was something Olivia would like? He needed to think of something quick. "Pizza," he blurted.

"Pizza?"

Heat creeped up his neck even though there was no one to notice just how on the spot he really felt. "Yes. Olivia likes pizza. See? We'd much rather you pick something that would suit your needs and the needs of your chef better."

"I'm sure Antonio can whip up an excellent pizza." Mr. Frederickson's voice sounded more amused than anything else. A chuckle filled the void between them. "There will be plenty of time to sample his cooking while you're here. I look forward to meeting this young woman you are bringing. Any person who prefers pizza over fine dining is someone after my own heart."

Isaac hung up the phone and exhaled, not realizing just how long he'd been holding his breath. It didn't matter what Olivia had put on her survey now. While they were with the Fredericksons, her new favorite food was pizza.

He raked a hand down his face and rubbed his jaw, then headed up the stairs. By the time he got up there, Olivia was telling one of the crew members where she wanted her luggage so she could change when she arrived. He took a seat nearby and pulled the tablet from his carry-on bag. Thank goodness her survey was electronic.

Isaac glanced up at Olivia briefly before he opened her

questionnaire and swiped through the questions until he found what he was looking for.

What is your favorite food? Hawaiian pizza.

He sucked in a breath and choked a little. "You've got to be kidding me." Isaac glanced up at Olivia as she headed toward him wearing those ridiculous slippers. "Did you fill out that questionnaire honestly?"

Her face scrunched up then she lifted a brow. "Of course I did. What reason would I have to lie?" She plopped into the chair across from him, then her focus shifted to the window.

Isaac turned the tablet around and pointed at the food question. "Your favorite food is Hawaiian pizza," he said flatly.

"So? Let me guess. Your favorite food is some ridiculous thing like lobster and caviar." She shuddered. "Who likes to eat snails anyway?"

His lips quirked up as he placed his device on the table between them. "First of all, no. My favorite food is not lobster nor caviar, and definitely not escargot."

She glanced at him.

"Escargot is snails," he explained.

Olivia wrinkled her nose. "I know that. Calling it a fancy name doesn't make it sound any nicer. I don't see the appeal to any of that."

"Looks like we agree on something." He chuckled. "But no, my favorite food is actually a good all-American cheeseburger."

Her expression went from disgust to surprise and her eyes swept over him like he'd told her he was an alien wearing a human suit. "You're lying."

Isaac laughed then used the exact words she'd thrown at him. "What reason would I have to lie?"

She rolled her eyes and returned her focus to the window. "You might just be trying to get on my good side."

His smile widened. "And telling you I like to eat burgers would do that?"

Olivia peeked at him. "Maybe."

"Oh yeah? Why's that?"

Her arms were folded over her chest and she gave him a wry smile. "Because it would mean you're not just some vapid stuffed shirt who looks down on everyone around him."

"And eating burgers equates to having good manners."

She snickered. "When you put it like that, *no*. But seriously, most people who have money tend to use it frivolously, don't they?"

"Actually, you might be surprised to find out that most people who have a great deal of wealth maintain it by being frugal." He settled into his seat. "And I can tell you that there are more kinds of burgers than those you find on the dollar menu. I've been to places where the burger costs as much as a good steak."

"Well, you've changed my mind then. I guess there's no reason I should like you after all." Her voice was light and her features were full of humor.

His gaze dipped to her smile, and he was overcome by a strange but pleasant sensation in his stomach. Isaac shook off the feeling and focused on her eyes again. "You sure don't mince words, do you?"

She shrugged. "Why should I? If someone doesn't like me, then it's a waste of time for both of us to try to develop a relationship." Her gaze darted away and a soft blush filled her cheeks. "Or even a friendship."

Her statement wasn't really surprising, but was impressive. Isaac studied her as if seeing a different person. The people he worked with on a daily basis were too concerned about what other people thought. Everything from their looks to their likes and views of the world were chosen by consensus. There was no telling how authentic they were.

Not the person who sat in front of him.

He'd only spent a short amount of time with her, but Olivia was the most genuine person he'd ever met. He might not like certain quirks she had, but at least he knew she was real. It'd be nice if more people were like her.

Chapter Eight

The plane ride was longer than she expected—though she'd never flown to New York before so her expectations were bound to be off. For hours Isaac swiped through his tablet, no doubt checking on his vast fortune. Every so often he'd glance in her direction.

At first she thought it was because he was disappointed she wasn't studying up on him. But after the tenth time and him not saying a word, she let out a heavy sigh. "What?"

Isaac lifted his gaze once more. "I didn't say anything."

"That's just it—you haven't said anything but you keep looking at me like I'm doing something wrong."

"Do *you* think you're doing something wrong?" His lips twitched at the corners and he turned back to his device.

"Don't do that."

"Don't do what?" This time his smile widened enough she could actually see it.

She waved at him. "You're doing that psychology thing on me. You're trying to make me say something or do something, aren't you?"

He peeked at her from beneath his brows then put his

tablet aside. "I don't have any idea what you're talking about."

"Is it because I'm not reading your little packet? Or because I'm wearing these?" She lifted her foot and waved a slipper at him.

Isaac's amused gaze shifted to the slipper and then back to her face. The way his eyes bore into hers made her heart stumble and she had to force herself to look away.

"Because if you have a problem with me, you might as well say it."

He shifted in his seat and she glanced at him once more. Isaac leaned over the table between them, a smile still on his face. "For the record, I already voiced my problems with your footwear, and we saw how well that went." He leaned back and appraised her. "The only thing on my mind, when it comes to this charade of ours, is that I need you to fulfill your side of the agreement. When we arrive, all eyes will be on you. It's not going to be easy. Any little mistake might be noticed, and your compensation depends on your performance. If you think you don't need to be reading that dossier, then by all means, spend your time the way you want."

Her stomach churned. He was right. She needed to brush up on some information about him so she wasn't put on the spot.

And yet...

The way Isaac had spoken to her just now had felt manipulative. He was trying to get her to do something by speaking to her in a way that would scare her. Olivia folded her arms. "If I can juggle multiple residents at Maple Gardens—knowing their routines, food preferences, allergies, medications"—she settled even more against her seat —"plus keep the admin side of things up to date, then I think I can handle whatever you throw at me. This is just a memorization game anyway." She turned to stare out at the surrounding sky. His attention unnerved her. She couldn't tell if it was because of fear that she wouldn't get her raise, or because his smile made little currents of electricity run through her body.

"Not really."

She shot a glance in his direction.

"This is more than knowing a bunch of facts about one another. We have to have chemistry."

Olivia arched a brow. "Chemistry? You can't be serious. It's not like we're engaged or anything."

"No, but we're dating. At least, as far as the investor I need on board is concerned. Like I said. We will be putting on a show. There will be eyes on us at all times. And if we slip up, then our story will start to crack." He leaned forward and his face grew serious as he poked the table with his forefinger. "There is more riding on this than you realize. Maple Gardens is the kind of place I want to see all over the country. We provide a service that many other retirement communities don't. I want to give more people access to this way of life because I see how much my mother has enjoyed it."

She blinked. When he put it that way, his desires were more admirable. Her brows creased and she adjusted herself so she sat straight up in her chair. "You realize that Maple Gardens is for the high paying client, right? The vast majority of people living in this country are living on a fixed income. I think you're going to find that what you want won't happen unless you make some changes."

He straightened, his expression contemplative. "I'm listening."

"Well, Maple Gardens is kind of like the gold standard

of retirement living. It's expensive. Yes, we provide excellent service, medical care, food, and lodging, but we also have a lot of space to roam. It's like its own little town within the community. And we cater for needs from those just easing into their later years through to younger folk like Izzie's mom. I mean, she's not even sixty but had an accident which affects her mobility and memory. I don't think you're going to reach the people who really need a place like that if prices can't be changed."

Amusement and something else filled his face. "What are you suggesting I do to fix that?"

She shrugged. "I don't know. There's a bottom line that has to be met, I guess."

"True." Isaac wasn't even trying to hide his smile anymore and at the moment all she wanted to do was wipe that smirk right off his face.

Olivia sat back in her seat. "I don't appreciate that you're making fun of me."

Isaac lifted one brow. "I'm not making fun of you."

"You're grinning at me like I'm an idiot who doesn't understand any of this." She gestured at him vaguely.

This time he actually chuckled. "I wasn't making fun of you," he repeated. "I find it fascinating that you could see what I was trying to attempt even though I never actually mentioned money."

She stilled—not just her body, but everything within it seemed to freeze. Her heart slowed, her lungs refused to expand as she waited for him to continue.

He settled into his seat and lifted his ankle to rest it on his knee. "Maple Gardens was designed by Bart's uncle Lawrence to be a retirement facility for the upper class. It serves its purpose well and we even offer funding to some residents who have a hard time affording it. Such as Izzie's mom. We receive several generous donations annually, which has allowed me to consider branching out to developing more retirement communities." He lifted his gaze to meet Olivia's. "You've hit the nail on the head. I don't want to create carbon copies of Maple Gardens. I want to use the same concepts to expand and provide similar living options to folks who might not otherwise be able to afford it. That is why Mr. Frederickson's investment is so important."

The pieces were starting to come together and the more Isaac spoke about what he wanted to do, the more attractive he was becoming. Olivia swallowed the lump in her throat. Was it possible she'd pegged him wrong?

"Opening new retirement communities will take a lot of money, and people like Mr. Frederickson are willing to not only invest, but make large donations—recurring ones, even. He's a man who has strong family values. And while I don't agree with his method of testing my character, I can't fault him for it."

And that's when he lost her. Olivia's brows pulled together. "So you're telling me that you want to expand Maple Gardens so that it can reach more people with varying financial backgrounds . . . by any means necessary."

"You say that like it's a bad thing. Look, what we offer at Maple Gardens is exemplary. Don't you think everyone should have access to that?"

"Yes," she drawled. "But at the cost of your morals? No."

His head reared back. "My morals? Who said my morals are at risk?"

She rolled her eyes. "What do you think Mr. Frederickson would think if he knew you lied about dating someone? Oh wait, you already know. That's why you hired me to help you keep your lie going. If you think your expansion of Maple Gardens is good enough to stand on its own, then there was no reason for you to have to lie to get an investor on board."

Isaac shook his head. "People have faults, Olivia. Everyone is prejudiced by one thing or another and Mr. Frederickson's is his need to see proof of something. I am a family man. I care for my mother and I provide for her. Do I have time to find a girlfriend and court her? No. But does that mean my business ideas are terrible?"

Are you being real? Or is this more manipulation?

"If you think Mr. Frederickson's flaw is that he can't see something without having proof, then your flaw is that you have to influence and control others so they see things exactly as you want them to. I hate to break this to you, but the world isn't black and white. I would wager that Mr. Frederickson would have heard you out if you had been persistent enough. You just needed to try a different course."

The amusement fled from his expression, and he frowned at her. "What do you think I'm doing? I'm finding another way to reach him when my first pitch fell on deaf ears. You have to agree that being in a relationship has nothing to do with running a business. My company is incredibly profitable and—"

"A man is only as good as his word." Her statement was all it took for the last fleeting happy spark to leave Isaac's eyes. She almost felt bad for putting him in his place like that. But it had to be done. People like Isaac needed to know that their desire to succeed was more important than their ethics. And he'd just shown her the biggest chink in his armor.

Olivia stood and headed for the back of the plane. She didn't know what she was going there to do. She could get her reading packet, or she could change her clothes and get ready for landing. The real reason she headed back there was to get away from Isaac and his now brooding expression.

The day she'd spilled her coffee on him, she might have relished the way she'd affected him. But now, she just felt like she'd lectured him into submission, and she couldn't grasp any joy from that moment.

He hadn't moved from his place. He hadn't even picked up his tablet to start reading again. Instead, he stared out the window with a sad, thoughtful look on his face.

Great. I broke him.

Okay, he probably wasn't broken. But if he didn't snap out of whatever funk he found himself in before the plane landed, she would have to carry more of the conversation with Mr. Frederickson, and she wasn't prepared for that.

The pilot's voice came over the intercom. "Attention, passengers. We will be preparing for landing in approximately thirty minutes . . ."

She'd better find something warmer for when they landed. And shoes.

Olivia reached for her suitcase from an overhead bin and it clattered to the floor, drawing the attention of both Isaac and the flight attendant. She flashed them an embarrassed smile and unzipped her suitcase. Her shoes should be right—

Oh no, oh no, oh no . . .

Her breath caught in her throat and her lungs seized up. She dug into the mess of wrinkled clothing, underwear, pajamas, and toiletries but she couldn't find anything to put on her feet. How could she have missed packing shoes? Olivia glanced at her fuzzy red slippers with despair then shot a look in Isaac's direction. He was going to be furious.

First she knocked him down a few pegs, and now she didn't have anything to wear but slippers.

Heat flashed across her face, chest, and neck and she slammed the suitcase shut. There might be a shoe store in the airport if she was lucky, but based on how the day had gone so far, she wasn't counting on it. They'd have to stop somewhere to buy some.

She shuffled toward him, her head hanging low. When she slumped into her seat, she avoided looking directly at him. "So . . . I have some bad news." Olivia met his gaze and, if it was possible, the heat in her face intensified.

Isaac glanced at her. "What."

Her lips pressed tightly before she blew out a breath through pursed lips. "You're not going to like this."

Chapter Nine

Isaac's first instinct was to tell her that he'd known this was going to happen. What did she expect when she lived in a glorified pig sty? Her clothes had been strewn all over the place. He wasn't even sure she packed winter gear. In fact, he had a sinking suspicion that if he went looking for her coat, he wouldn't have found one of those either.

He stared at her, watching as she winced, preparing for him to let her have it.

If he hadn't been feeling depressed, he might have done just that.

But at the moment he had more things to worry about. She had been completely right. He'd sacrificed something —however small—in order to achieve the bigger picture. And from the moment she pointed it out, his stomach had knotted and he felt like he was going to throw up.

Isaac let out a sigh and pulled out his phone.

She peered at him, shifting in her seat as he got to work typing a message for his assistant. "What are you doing? Didn't you hear me? I didn't bring any shoes. The only thing I have is what I'm wearing."

His gaze flitted to her and then down to his phone as he pushed the send button. "I heard you."

"Well? Aren't you going to get mad? Yell at me for making a mistake? Something?"

"Do you want me to yell at you?"

She snapped her mouth shut and shook her head. "No. But based on how I just put you in your place, I figured . . ." She shrugged.

"In spite of what you might think of me, I'm not some monster who enjoys making people feel bad."

She flinched—or maybe it was just his imagination.

"Did I assume something like this would happen? Yes. Is yelling at you going to do either of us any good? No."

When she finally spoke, her voice was soft and he almost didn't understand what she asked. "What are we going to do? I doubt you want our first impression as a couple to be me dressed like this. I'd need an iron before wearing anything in my suitcase."

Isaac lifted his phone and offered her a smile that he didn't really feel. "My assistant is on it."

"Isn't he still in Georgia?"

He placed his phone back in his pocket as the flight attendant came by to make sure everyone was prepared for landing. Olivia put her seatbelt on and, once the attendant was gone, he folded his arms and gazed out the window. "My assistant will contact a clothing store and make sure we won't be disturbed while you get what you need."

Her eyes rounded and her mouth dropped open. Then she shook her head vehemently and the flush from earlier returned to her face. "I don't have money for that. I—" The color deepened in her cheeks and she looked away. Her voice was just above a whisper. "I'm barely making rent as it is."

His chest tightened and he nearly unbuckled his seat to lean over the table to comfort her. But based on the way she was acting right now, he didn't think she would appreciate the attention. Olivia was a proud woman. She wasn't about to take handouts from a guy she clearly despised.

Isaac gazed out the window, acting as if he didn't notice her discomfort, though it tore him up inside. "Don't worry about it. I'll write it off as a business expense."

"But—"

This time he met her gaze steadily. "This isn't one of those things you can negotiate about with me. We're on a business trip and sometimes that means we have to purchase certain amenities. You can't exactly go wandering the snow-covered streets in fuzzy slippers. We'll get you something sensible, and I don't want to hear another word about it." He settled back against his seat and closed his eyes. There was no point in looking at her. He knew that she wasn't likely to be happy with him putting his foot down.

You need to deal with it. I'm still the boss.

The plane eased into a downward descent, and he gripped the arm rests. No matter how often he'd ridden on a plane, this was the worst part. He hated the way his body felt like it was going down while his stomach no longer conformed to gravity.

A distinct click hit his ears and his eyes flew open just as Olivia moved around the table to take the seat beside him. "What on earth—" He watched with anxiety as Olivia settled in, buckled her seatbelt, then placed her hand over his. His gaze dipped to where she held his hand and his heart leaped into his throat.

He wasn't reacting to her. He was still reacting to his irrational fear of being on a plane when it shifted to a downward trajectory. Why was she holding his hand? The question was on the tip of his tongue, but then she smiled at him. It wasn't a flirty smile, nor was it full of pity. It was a genuine kind of smile and it made his heart race just a little faster.

Olivia sat back against her chair and closed her eyes, not saying a single word. It was better that way. They'd had a few hard discussions during their plane ride.

The aircraft landed without incident and when the plane slowed, Olivia leaned over him to stare out the window. Tiny flakes floated from the sky and the airport was covered in Christmas lights. It was always strange to come to the colder states this time of year. He'd nearly forgotten that the holidays were right around the corner.

Olivia stood, hovering over him, her perfume causing a pleasant fire to burn within him. He was almost disappointed when she moved away and sat back in her seat. "I've never seen so much snow." She practically glowed, from her eyes to her crooked grin. "I love Christmas time."

Isaac glanced once more out the window then back to her. "Really?"

She seemed surprised at his question. "Of course, don't you?"

He rubbed his jaw and chuckled. "Somehow I pegged you as the type of person who hated the commercialism of the holiday."

Olivia let out a soft laugh. "Yeah, I could see that." This softer side of her was really getting to him. She wasn't what he'd expected her to be. She lifted a shoulder and rubbed her arm. "I suppose I do still hate that sort of thing. But there's more to the holiday than all the stuff people spend money on. It's not about the parades and gifts. It's about being able to be with people you care about. I throw this annual Christmas Eve party every year. I invite everyone I know, and we have cookies, play games, and sing karaoke." She laughed again. "It's the best."

"Don't you spend time with your family?"

She shook her head. "Besides the expense of traveling to them, my parents are usually off visiting some warmer location. It's not really conducive to my lifestyle to travel." Olivia broke eye contact. Then she got to her feet and only briefly glanced in his direction. "Don't we have somewhere important to be? And I need my luggage."

"The luggage will follow us."

Without arguing, she headed toward the front of the plane. He scrambled to his feet and hurried after her. "But if you had the means to visit your family, would you?"

Her eyes flitted to meet his over her shoulder. "Sure. But that's not how it is." Olivia's features softened and she slowed, turning to face him, causing him to almost bump into her. "You know, you should come to my party this year."

Isaac stiffened. "I should?"

"Why not? I already invited Bart and Izzie. You're friends with them. What's one more person?" She turned again and faced the exit. A gust of frigid air blew snowflakes into the plane and she let out a squeal, turning into him as he stepped closer. Instinctively, his arms encircled her. Neither one of them had the proper outerwear, and just standing here with her like this offered them both additional warmth.

Olivia tilted her chin and her laughing eyes turned serious as they stood, frozen, as if in a painting. She fit within his arms like he'd always thought a woman should. Her floral scent reactivated that strange tight feeling in his stomach. His gaze shifted to her full, pink lips and he dipped his head closer to her.

Her lashes fluttered and she attempted to pull away from him, but the back of her heel met the edge of the stairs and she sucked in a gasp. He held to her tightly and let out a strained laugh. What was he thinking? He couldn't kiss her. Not like this, not here. She was his employee. There were so many things wrong with even considering stealing a kiss from those soft, velvety lips.

Isaac cleared his throat and stepped back after making sure she was steady. She shot him one more glance and carefully turned to head down the steps toward the waiting limo. Chills swept down his back as he watched her retreating form. He hadn't been prepared for his body to react in such a way.

Olivia wasn't his type. The way she kept her apartment made it perfectly clear he wouldn't be able to handle being close to her.

If Bart had been here, he would have laughed in Isaac's face. He might have even attempted to get the two of them together. But Bart was wrong, and so was that short moment of misjudgment.

Isaac headed down the stairs, followed by their crew, who were busy with the luggage. The driver of the car held the door open for Olivia, then waited for Isaac to climb in beside her. She scooted to the far side, putting as much distance between them as possible. Once the door was shut, she folded her legs up beneath herself and gave him a small smile. "Where did your assistant say we should go?"

He pulled out his phone and opened up an email from his assistant. "Looks like the Fredericksons live on the upper east side. We'll be going to a clothing store near them."

She nodded and shifted her focus out the window. *I'll be Home for Christmas* played quietly on the radio and the snow flurries outside grew thicker with each passing moment. The gray-blue sky almost matched the hue of Olivia's eyes.

Nope.

He needed to stop thinking about her eyes, her smile, and the way her perfume made his insides churn. Olivia was a means to an end and he wasn't even sure she'd be able to fulfill her side of the agreement. One wrong move and everything he'd planned would fail.

Their conversation from earlier came back like a punch to the gut. He'd never admit it to her, but he hated the way she'd pointed out his dishonesty. No matter how he tried to look at it, he couldn't come up with a solution.

He was stuck. There was no way Mr. Frederickson would even consider investing in Maple Gardens if he found out that Isaac had lied. This had been one big mistake but it would be too costly to backtrack.

Isaac would just have to promise himself that he'd never put himself in this position again. It had been out of character in the first place—a move of desperation.

He shot another look in Olivia's direction. Not many people would call him out on his mistakes. She was different, intriguing, and someone he actually wanted to get to know better—not just because she was supposed to be his fake girlfriend. He wanted to get to know Olivia better because, for the first time in his life, he might have found someone who was worth it.

Chapter Ten

She was in trouble.

More than in trouble, Olivia was doomed.

She'd gone and opened her big mouth and said way too much. She'd pointed out her boss's weaknesses like they were imperfections in a piece of artwork that made him somehow unworthy. Then she'd gone soft when she'd seen his blatant anxiety. For someone who used a private jet so often, he sure didn't act like it.

It was hard to watch him struggle with it, even though *he* thought he hid it well. And before she realized what she was doing, she was sitting beside him, holding his hand. What else could she have done?

Stayed put. That's what.

Olivia wasn't here to baby him. She was here to do a job and she had overstepped so many times she wouldn't be surprised if he walked away from their agreement.

But he needed her. That much was clear. The only question was whether she could push him so far that he would find a way out.

That thought didn't sit well in her stomach. And it

wasn't just the promotion. She'd seen a softer side to him—one that made him seem not so bad. Isaac might be a wealthy billionaire who could do whatever he wanted and get away with it unscathed, but he was still human and there were parts of him that called to her.

Dang it.

Her mother had always said her kind heart would get her in trouble one day. This was one of those times.

Olivia placed her head in her palm and sighed. For all she knew, she might be too late. Once a train started moving forward, it was far more difficult to make it reverse.

Yep. Sometimes it was just best to ride the crazy train to the next station and see what the damage was.

Right now, it appeared she was developing *something* for him. But just what that was, she had no clue. She'd taken a job at Maple Gardens because she was good at caring for people. It was possible that this situation would turn out similar to the few close friendships she'd been blessed with.

The vehicle came to a stop outside of a strip of elegant old buildings. The lights in the display windows shone brightly on the mannequins, showing off the bright colors for the winter season. Beyond the display, the store lights toward the front were partially shut off.

She shot a concerned look in Isaac's direction. "Are you sure they're open? They look pretty closed to me."

Isaac leaned over her to get a better view out her window and she was hit in the face with his irresistible cologne. "My assistant just said that if we came here, we wouldn't get any trouble from people looking to take tabloid photos. The store owners promised privacy."

"Does that happen often?" Her head was cloudy but she managed to get a couple words out despite feeling like

Isaac's scent was blocking anything from traveling along her brain's synapses.

He shrugged as he settled back in his seat. "It really depends on the city and who I'm with." His eyes swept over her less-than-ideal outfit and one side of his mouth lifted into an amused smirk. "They'd have a heyday with you."

She gasped. "What is that supposed to mean?"

One brow lifted. "You didn't exactly bring clothes that are appropriate for this social setting."

"Maybe it's the other way around. Have you considered that? *Maybe* people would be surprised to find out that you're with someone as unique and amazing as me."

"Oh yes, I'm sure that's it." Sarcasm dripped from his tone and her mouth dropped open.

She'd show him. There might not be a lot of things she was really good at but cleaning up was one area where she excelled. She had an eye for fashion. She just didn't have the money to put it all together.

Olivia stared out the window as the driver came around to open the door for her. He held his hand out to her and she accepted. He was dressed in a fancy suit, much like Isaac. A few people wandering down the street gave her some strange looks.

Maybe Isaac had a point. She wasn't in Georgia anymore. But the problem wasn't the place. It was who she was with. If she had seen someone dressed in fuzzy slippers climb out of a limo, she would have thought it strange, too.

Well, that depended on her mood.

There were times when she might have thought a billionaire wearing fuzzy slippers was on point. They'd made it. They shouldn't have to conform to what society wanted them to be. But right now, that wasn't where her thoughts were.

She'd never admit it to Isaac, but she was almost embarrassed by her outfit. The tattered jeans, the oversized sweater that draped off one shoulder, and yes, the slippers.

Not my best work.

Isaac emerged from the vehicle and came up to stand beside her. He placed a gentle hand on the small of her back. Olivia shivered, but not because of his touch. No, she was just cold. Just because he was handsome and had money and sometimes could act like a real human being didn't mean she was going to develop a crush on him.

That would be ridiculous.

She took a few quick steps to put distance between herself and Isaac—until she could no longer feel the warmth emanating from him.

Isaac quickened his steps and made it to the door right before she did. He pulled on the handle and motioned for her to enter. She mumbled, "Thank you."

He gave her a curt nod and they moved farther into the shop. Out of nowhere, a young man in a nice suit materialized. "Welcome to FashioneNYNY, Mr. Spencer. It will be my pleasure to assist you today." His gaze shifted to Olivia and his eyebrows rose almost to his hairline.

Isaac smiled. "Wonderful."

Olivia huffed. These two were peas in a pod. It was like they had a secret society where only the upper-class could receive the respect that everyone deserved to get. She folded her arms. Why did everything have to be based on someone's looks?

The man stepped closer. "This must be Miss Todd. If you would come with—"

"Thank you, but I think I can handle picking out my own clothes."

She got a warning look from Isaac but she ignored it

and held out her hand. He stared at her open palm, his brows furrowing.

"Your credit card. I'm going to need it to get my things."

He stared at her like she was crazy, but there was something that hovered just beneath the surface. He was amused by her. Well at least that was something. Isaac dug out his card but instead of giving it to her, he held it out to the salesman. "She can get whatever she likes."

She snorted. "Are you sure you want to agree to that?"

Isaac chuckled. "I'm sure you can't do too much damage here."

"Is that a challenge?"

He moved closer to her and his voice lowered. "We're going to be here for a few days. While we're here, you're my girlfriend. I'll be expected to show you off. Perhaps you should worry less about what I'm going to spend and more about the first impressions you'll be making."

Goosebumps rose on her arms as his husky voice slipped and tantalized the inner workings of her ears. Her first instinct was to pick out hideous outfits, and she was fully prepared to do so until she started wandering through the racks on her own.

There were some really cute clothes here. And the majority of the things she looked at had price tags that were in the hundreds. She'd never be able to afford the name brand stuff at this store.

She had two choices.

Olivia could take advantage of a free shopping spree or she could pick out the most ridiculous outfits just to prove a point.

Both options were incredibly tempting, which said a lot about her personality. Regardless of which one she chose, she was being selfish, which only served to make her more irritated.

She heaved a sigh as she wandered through the racks of winter coats. There was one that caught her eye and she pulled it from the rack. The exterior was white with gorgeous faux fur around the neck. Inside, the lining was a different material. Softer. When she glanced at the price she nearly choked. After tax, the coat would be over a thousand dollars. That money could cover two months' rent where she was staying. Or at least it could have before the prices went up.

"You've got a good eye."

Olivia jumped and quickly put the coat back. She spun around to find the salesman watching her. Isaac was nowhere to be found. Figured. He probably had some kind of work thing to do. She nodded, eyeing the coat once more. "It is a very beautiful coat."

"Shall I have it taken to the front for you?"

"What? No."

He gave her a funny look. "Is it not to your liking?"

"It's perfect. But I don't think Mr.—my boyfriend would appreciate me spending so much on a coat I'll only use while I'm here." She couldn't rationalize using it back home. Besides, it didn't get nearly that cold where she lived. "I'll keep looking. Thanks."

He nodded but didn't leave his place.

"Must you do that?"

The man lifted a brow. "Pardon?"

"That hovering. Are you required to watch me shop? Are you worried I'm going to steal something?"

"Of course not, ma'am. I'm here if you need any assistance."

She groaned. There wasn't a good chance that he'd

leave her alone. This was his job and he certainly got paid more than she did to just stand around while people bought clothes. Olivia spun on her heel and made a beeline for the casual wear. There were a lot more options to pick from than she'd expected. She ended up settling on a pair of dress pants, a beautiful knit sweater, a casual dress, a gorgeous long skirt, a pair of jeans, and a few blouses. She picked up a pair of stylish, white snow boots and dumped the items into the man's waiting arms. Without looking at the price, she added a double-breasted red coat that had a strap to tie around the waist. "There. Take that up to the front and I'll pick out my evening wear."

He nodded and finally left her in peace.

Olivia didn't know what Isaac was about to spend, but every single thing she'd picked out was to her taste. Even better for him, they would make her look like she belonged with a guy like him.

Her eyes landed on a bright red dress that had been embellished with small crystals. She plucked it from the rack and slipped into the dressing room. It glittered like the twinkling lights that had been strung up on a Christmas tree in the front of the store. The sleeves were long and the back swooped low with a single strap that ran horizontal just above her lower back. The floor-length dress had a slit all the way up her left leg to her mid-thigh. It was the perfect dress to make Isaac's mouth fall to the floor.

She grinned wickedly. This dress was amazing—if she had anywhere special to go in the foreseeable future, she'd happily pull this from her closet.

Olivia didn't even want to look at the price tag. She didn't want to feel guilty over the money Isaac was spending on her. But at the same time, she couldn't deny the flutters that erupted in her chest at thought of Isaac's reaction when she emerged for the Christmas party at Mr. Frederickson's home.

"Miss Todd? Are you all right in there?"

She started, and a squeak slipped from her lips. "Yes." Her voice cracked. "I'm fine. Just finishing up here and I'll be right out."

"Is there anything—"

"No," she blurted. "There's nothing you can do for me, thank you."

She quickly got out of the dress and draped it over her arm. When she emerged, the salesman was right there. Olivia let out a yelp, then glared at the man. "You know, not everyone likes to be stalked while they're shopping."

"Actually, that's a common misconception." His tone was serious. So was his face. She couldn't tell if he was joking with her or if he was being sarcastic. Either way, she was at a loss for how to respond.

Olivia shoved the dress at him and stalked off to find some casual shoes. It was a good thing she didn't have a lot of money. He was only doing his job but being followed around as she selected clothes was unsettling. Was this really how the rich and famous lived?

Chapter Eleven

Isaac glanced up from his phone as Olivia swiftly hurried toward the front of the store. "Did you find everything you need?" His eyes swept over her and landed on her slippers. "You're still wearing *those*?" While it was oddly humorous, the time had come to get serious. She needed to be in proper footwear when they arrived.

"Yes, they're mine."

He was about to say something when the salesman appeared with her dress.

"Ma'am, you failed to select a pair of shoes for this evening wear. They are the same size as the casual pairs you chose. "I've taken it upon myself to gather three options that work best with your dress if you'd—"

"I trust your judgment. Pick whichever one you think is best." Olivia turned to Isaac. "Can I go out to the car now? I'd rather not spend another second in here."

His brows furrowed. "Was it really so bad?" He would have thought that she would enjoy picking out some decent clothes. Had he been wrong?

"Maybe I'm just tired and want to have a place to sit

down in peace where a man isn't hovering over me like a vulture."

He chuckled as he got to his feet. "Of course you can. Mr. Jenkins might not notice you—"

"I am fully capable of opening doors all by myself, Isaac."

"I didn't say you weren't—"

"And guess what? I can tie my own shoes too." She lifted her chin and headed for the door.

"That will be two-thousand, nine-hundred, and forty-seven dollars and eighty-one cents."

Isaac nodded and moved toward the counter as the man held out his card.

"*What?*" Olivia materialized beside him. "You're kidding. It can't be that much. I know that the dress was expensive, but—" Her eyes dipped to where the salesman was folding a white coat. She reached over the counter and took the coat from his hands. "Oh no, I said not this one. I don't need a coat that costs so much."

Isaac gently removed the garment from her grasp and returned it to the poor salesman who stared at Olivia like she'd lost her mind. "It's okay, Olivia. I asked him to pick one out when he showed me the jacket you chose."

"And the red jacket will more than suffice for me while I'm here. I don't need another one."

"That red jacket is a great choice when it's warmer, but I have a feeling we'll be out in the cold while we're here. You don't know New York winters like I do." If Mr. Frederickson wanted them to go ice-skating or to wander to a Broadway musical, there was a good chance she'd freeze to death in that jacket.

He wanted to tell her she'd look beautiful in the white

coat but her eyes were furious as they drilled into him. Why did he have to find her assertiveness so attractive?

"You're not going to win this argument, so you might want to put those daggers you're staring at me away. Sheathe them for another time."

She didn't move for a full minute. Or at least that was how it felt. Despite the anger in them, or because of it, those eyes drew him in until his heart began to thud and then his gaze dropped to her lips.

Olivia puffed out a heavy breath and strode toward the door.

Did you know I wanted to kiss you then?

When Isaac turned, the salesman was staring at him with a disapproving expression.

Isaac chuckled. "She's very independent. She doesn't like me spending money on her."

That was all it took for the salesman's features to relax with understanding. "Thank you for shopping at Fashione-NYNY. Would you like me to assist you with your items?"

Isaac shook his head and scooped up the shopping bags. Thank you for your help. And for helping me with the coat." He gave the man a knowing smile. "I'm sure she'll love it."

He headed outside. His driver stood beside the vehicle, ready to take his bags and open his door. Isaac gave him a nod of appreciation and climbed inside to find Olivia glowering at him.

"Okay, now that was too much."

"Was it?" he murmured dryly as he pulled out his phone to check his messages. "I've spent more money on a suit."

Isaac didn't bother looking at her. He could tell by the drastic drop in temperature that she wasn't thrilled to hear this. Well, it wasn't her money and he could do what he wanted with it. His original motive was about her being properly dressed to make the right impression. But now there was something else. She might not have enjoyed the sales-man's attention but she had wonderful taste and had risen to the challenge of updating her holiday attire on short notice.

The driver glanced over his shoulder. "Will there be any other stops this afternoon, Mr. Spencer?"

"No. We're expected at the Frederickson home. They've prepared dinner."

Again, he felt the animosity coming from the seat beside him.

Isaac sighed. "Is there anything you'd like to say to me?"

She drew in a quick breath but offered nothing.

He shot a quick look at the back of Jenkins's head then raised the window partition that would separate the driver from the passengers. Once they were alone, Isaac put his phone away and faced Olivia. "Once we arrive, you will be on display. You will be the face of Maple Gardens. Mr. Fred-erickson might be looking for a reason why he shouldn't invest in the company."

Her expression softened and she almost looked worried.

"Everything will be fine. You just need to make sure to watch what you say and how you act. Go with the flow."

Olivia wrinkled her nose. "It's like you're telling me I have to be some kind of Stepford wife."

"I suppose it's a good thing we're not married then, huh?" He held back a smile. "Once this week is over, we can 'break up' and no one will be the wiser. Do you think you can handle that?"

"I'm here, aren't I?"

"That right there. That's what I'm talking about. It's more than the words that come out of your mouth. It's the tone of voice you use. You can't make anyone feel like they're beneath you."

"Isn't that what wealthy people do to people like me?"

Is that what you really believe?

Isaac's mouth dropped open. He'd made a mistake. Olivia wasn't the right fit and it was too late to change anything.

Her straight, irritated face broke into a wide smile and she threw her head back and laughed. "You're too serious. Geez. I've worked in hospitality. And I work with our residents. Don't you think that I know how to talk to people? By the time this week is over, you might even believe that I'm in love with you." She folded her arms and sat back, then stared out the window.

"If you could make me believe *that*, I'll double your salary."

"Don't make promises you can't keep."

"Okay, you're right. I wouldn't be able to do that. But let's make this interesting."

Olivia's whole body stiffened. It was clear that she wanted to look at him. She was curious. But she wasn't willing to bring herself to meet his gaze.

"If you do so well that everyone we meet believes you're head over heels in love with me, I'll pay your rent for a year."

That got her attention. He'd hit a chord. Olivia turned around and stared at him with wide eyes. "You're not serious."

"I'm dead serious. As much as I hate to admit it, Mr. Frederickson's insistence that I am in a committed relationship is a very real concern of mine. I can't afford to fail this week. I'm willing to give you whatever is going to help you get through this week."

The look on her face either said that she thought he was crazy or that she didn't believe him. Maybe both.

"I know I've already told you I'd fast-track your raise. You don't have to believe me. Maybe I'm showing my hand—"

"You're absolutely showing your hand. You don't even know how much I pay for rent a month."

He shrugged. "I'm CEO of several real-estate holdings. I've got a pretty good idea of what I'm offering."

"And all I have to do is convince everyone that I'm deeply in love with you? Do I have to convince you, too?"

Isaac chuckled. "I don't think you'll be that good."

Olivia pressed her lips together tightly, her gaze shifting away. It was a lot to consider. He understood that. This was a strange situation in the first place. But if he wanted to maintain control, he needed to account for all variables. Even his own unreliable feelings about her.

The limo came to a stop and the window that separated them from the driver came down. "We've arrived, sir."

Isaac glanced at Olivia and found her looking at him. This was it. They were at the Frederickson house. It was now or never.

She smiled and gave him a quick nod. That was all he needed.

Olivia pulled out her new boots and the new coat then put them on.

When the driver opened the door, Isaac stepped out. Olivia scooted toward the edge of the seat and he held out his hand to her. She placed her long, slender fingers within his.

An electrical current flowed between them as their eyes met and he pulled her to her feet. He was a bundle of nerves. It wasn't just the investment that was on the line. It was his reputation, too.

Olivia tugged her hand free and wrapped her arms around his neck. He stiffened, his brows pulling together as he tried to make sense of what she was up to. Was this what she'd been referring to when she said she could make him believe she had feelings for him?

He couldn't pull his eyes away from her and when she lifted her fingers up to the hair near his temple, a chill rippled down his spin. He couldn't remember the last time he'd had a woman so close to him. She tilted her head, her lips forming a soft smile just before she stood on her toes and lightly brushed her lips against his. The electricity from before ignited into something far more powerful and his nerves called out for more. He slipped his arms around her waist and was about to pull her closer when a voice stopped him.

"Ah, Mr. Spencer. It's wonderful to see you again. I trust your flight was agreeable?"

Isaac turned to find Mr. Frederickson standing a few feet away and slightly behind him. He'd been in perfect view from Olivia's perspective. She must have seen him coming and did what she had to in order to fulfill her side of the arrangement.

His heart sunk, which didn't make a lick of sense.

He wasn't interested in Olivia that way.

Is she beautiful?

Gorgeous.

Does she have a strong personality?

An understatement. Her personality was closer to a red flag than something he needed on his wish list.

Sense of humor? Ambition? Kind heart?

Yes to all of the above.

But none of that meant he should be interested in her that way. Even if her lightest touch started a small blaze deep inside. Isaac flung his wayward thoughts aside and forced a smile, while Olivia kept her arms noosed around his neck. "Our trip went well, thank you. But Olivia here misplaced her snow boots so we made a stop in town to pick some up."

Mr. Frederickson looked down and his smile grew. "Well, she has excellent taste. But we knew that already, because she picked you."

The tightness in Isaac's chest returned with a vengeance. Olivia didn't pick him. And if he'd had more time, he wouldn't have picked her.

Get out of your head, Spencer. You knew this would happen. Suck it up and deal with it like you would any other business arrangement.

Isaac pulled away from Olivia, but she followed his movements.

He was secretly thrilled at how well she was taking what he'd said to heart. Her hand slipped through his arm and she rested her cheek against his shoulder. "It's a pleasure to meet you, Mr. Frederickson. Isaac has told me so much about you."

The man laughed. "All good things, I hope."

She nodded. "Of course. He holds you in very high regard."

Mr. Frederickson beamed, the compliment showing in his expression. "Well, let's get out of the cold and I'll show you to your room. I hope it's okay that you share one. I have several guests coming and going this week. You understand."

Both Isaac and Olivia didn't move. Isaac's whole body went cold. Sharing a room. He hadn't even considered the sleeping arrangements. What would Olivia say to this? Would she insist that she needed more money due to this unforeseen bump in the road? He had to speak up otherwise Mr. Frederickson would think something was amiss.

Olivia beat him to it. "We'll happily accept any hospitality you show us."

Mr. Frederickson glanced from Isaac to Olivia and back again. "I'm sure I don't have to tell you this, but she's a keeper. You take care of this one, Spencer."

"I intend to."

Chapter Twelve

It was a darn good thing Olivia had acted in three of her high school's musicals when she was younger. She knew exactly what kind of body language would be expected at this stage in the visit. And the moment she saw Mr. Frederickson heading their way, she bolted into action.

There is only one problem.

She hadn't expected to feel anything when she kissed him.

It was a glorified stage kiss after all.

Maybe it was the way his hands came around her waist almost possessively that had pushed her over the edge. Or it could be how he stared at her like she was some kind of ethereal creature. Either way, that fake kiss had felt *very* real to her.

And now she was in trouble.

Her thoughts continued to swirl as she considered the implications of sharing a room with Isaac. He had reminded her that they needed to put on a show for all to see. What would their host have said if she had told him she needed her own room?

As far as she could tell, he might have two reactions.

The first was that they were ungrateful for his generosity, thereby putting a sour taste in his mouth toward Maple Gardens.

The other reaction—he might not believe Isaac's story.

Well, that reaction was less likely. He didn't know anything about Isaac's home life. She'd only met Mr. Frederickson, but he didn't seem the suspicious type.

Regardless, she wasn't about to rock the boat. Not when she had a year's rent on the line.

Right now, she needed to focus on keeping the walls around her heart intact. Isaac was handsome and he was generous. But he was also a jerk—she couldn't let him overthrow the way she felt about him just because he got her some pretty clothes.

She stepped forward to follow Mr. Frederickson when he motioned at his house, but Isaac held her back until the older man was a few yards away.

"What was that?" he hissed between clenched teeth.

"What?" she whispered. "We have to be gracious guests. If he offers us a room—"

"No. The kiss. What did you do that for?"

She spun to face him, her eyes dancing with mischief. "Oh, that. I thought that's what you wanted." It took everything in her power to maintain a level tone. Under no circumstances was he to realize that the kiss had stirred something within her. She'd never hear the end of it.

"We never discussed public displays of affection."

"No, but you clearly want everyone around us to believe we're in love. Or did I misunderstand you?" There was a tremor in her voice she couldn't shake and she prayed he didn't notice.

"Of course I want them to—"

"Then you're going to have to deal with PDAs. It's a fact that people who are in a serious relationship kiss, hug, and stuff. If you can't handle that, then you might as well—"

"Who said I couldn't handle it?" he snapped.

This was a side of him she hadn't experienced before. "You just seem a little agitated." This was actually one thing she could use to her advantage. If he was busy being annoyed, he wouldn't notice how he affected her.

"That's because I am. I need to be prepared for when you do something like that. Otherwise. . ." He trailed off as if he couldn't complete his thought.

"What? Are you saying you can't handle being kissed without warning?" She couldn't keep the teasing out of her tone. It was actually kind of cute, the way he was making a big deal about this, only it would have been better if he was making a big deal because he felt the same unsettling stirrings that she had.

"Wouldn't you say the same about yourself?"

Uh oh. Had he noticed? No. That was impossible. She just had to play it cool. Olivia shrugged. "I'm fine with it."

"Really?" he said with disbelief.

"Really. It's just a kiss, Isaac. No one is asking you to marry me."

"So if I were to kiss you right now without asking, you'd be okay with it."

She shrugged again. "Like I said. It doesn't bother me."

Without warning, he grasped her by her upper arms and pulled her close. His lips crushed against hers, pulling the energy right from her body with a soul-stealing kiss. Isaac's mouth roved over hers, teasing her, exploring the curves of her lips. This was nothing like the chaste kiss she'd given him. It was so much more.

She knew the kiss wouldn't last long, but she felt like

she lived several lifetimes in those few moments. Chills coursed through her body, betraying her mind and tantalizing her heart. Goosebumps lifted on her arms and it wasn't because of the cold. Her lashes fluttered, and she stared at Isaac in shock when he pulled back.

Isaac held her at arm's length, a smirk touching his lips. "See? Doesn't that feel like a violation of some sort? You can't tell me that you want me to do that when you're not prepared for it."

Shock and longing were immediately doused with what could only be compared to a bucket of ice water. Olivia's hands clenched into fists at her sides. "You did that to prove a point?"

"Why else would I do it?" He folded his arms, that infuriating smirk still plastered to his face. He chuckled and tilted his head. "Why are you mad?"

His eyes danced with amusement and, not for the first time, she wanted to slap him.

Her voice lowered into a hiss. "There's a difference between a random kiss to make your audience believe we're in a relationship, per your instructions, and a kiss that is meant to be hurtful to the person you're delivering it to." She hated how much it hurt to realize he'd only kissed her to make her uncomfortable.

But even more than that, she hated how much she wanted more.

If she couldn't get a handle on these hormonal reactions, this week was going to be the longest one of her life.

Olivia brushed past him and strode toward the house. He reached out and caught the sleeve of her coat, stopping her from getting very far. She stared at where he held her, then lifted her gaze to his face. If she cried she would never forgive herself. "What?" The word escaped through clenched teeth.

"Are you—mad at me?" The humor was gone from both his voice and his eyes. His brows were creased and he didn't seem to stand as tall as he had. Once again, the wall had come up between them. Those little moments that they had shared not even a few hours ago seemed to have dissolved and they were back at square one.

She took in a deep breath, reminding herself that he had hired her, and some of the things he'd said actually made sense. She probably should have given him some kind of warning. Letting out her sigh, she shook her head. "No. I'm not mad. Just . . . please think about why you're doing something before you do it."

The heat from his gaze seemed to seep into her skin, causing the churning in her stomach to continue. In a perfect world—no, in a fairytale world—this thing they started might actually work out. They could be that couple who hated each other until they fell in love.

But this is no fairytale.

She gently tugged her arm away from him and nodded toward the building. "Come on. I'm starving."

The sidewalk salt crunched under Olivia's new boots with each step she took. She could hear Isaac following her, his closeness doing nothing to improve her mood. They got to the front door where Mr. Frederickson waited. He smiled at them both and gestured toward someone dressed like a butler from nineteenth century England.

"Larson will show you to your room so you can deposit your things and then you're invited to come down for dinner. Your luggage will be up shortly."

Larson nodded but he didn't say anything. He looked to be in his fifties, his hair and beard neatly trimmed. He turned on his heel and strode toward a grand staircase draped with garland and oversized Christmas balls.

Olivia stopped in her tracks, getting her first proper look at this place. Her head tilted back as she took in the stairs, the chandelier, and the vaulted ceilings. This kind of place was something she thought only existed in the movies. Never had she imagined that she'd be a guest in a residence like this.

Whoever Mr. Frederickson was, he appeared to be really important.

Isaac nudged her, his shoulder bumping into hers. "Come on," he whispered. "Don't want to keep him waiting." He moved past her and she followed.

They wandered up the stairs and headed down a hall where Larson opened a door and held out a hand with a flourish. While Isaac thanked him, Olivia entered the room. A high ceiling and a large, king-sized bed were the focal points. There was a large dresser, a chaise lounge, and two other doors. Both were open, revealing the interiors.

She moved toward the closet first. It was empty apart from two luxurious dressing gowns. There was plenty of room for her things ten times over. Next she moved to the bathroom. A massive walk-in shower was encased in glass. Overhead was a rain showerhead. Beside the shower was a soaker tub, and the vanity had his and hers sinks. She could fit her entire kitchen in this bathroom.

Olivia moved back to the doorway and nearly bumped into Isaac. The tension still hovered between them from their argument—if that's what it had been. She looked away, placing her hands behind her back and shifting her weight from one foot to the other.

He leaned against the doorjamb and she couldn't tell

what was worse—that he looked angry, or that his smoldering stare made her want him to hold her again.

She cleared her throat and peeked over his shoulder. "Shouldn't we . . ."

Isaac didn't move. His eyes narrowed and his jaw ticked from side to side. Just when she thought she might spontaneously combust from the heat of his gaze, he spoke. "I think I should apologize."

Her eyes shot up to meet his. She had to be imagining this, right? That was the only thing that made sense. Isaac Spencer never apologized. More specifically, he hadn't apologized for the time he spilled coffee all over her shirt. The shock must have been clearly visible, because he looked away and let out a small cough.

"I shouldn't have kissed you like that. It was unprofessional at worst, and at best—" His eyes darted to meet hers then away again. He let out a sigh. "You have every right to feel safe and I need to make sure you do. Perhaps before we head down to eat, we set up some ground rules."

Her hands dropped to her sides and her heart hammered. What would he say if she told him she didn't need ground rules? That it was tempting to pretend this whole thing was real instead of the other way around? Instead, she nodded. "Okay. What are you suggesting? Some new contract? Do I have to sign something?" Yes, there was sarcasm in her tone, but, again, he didn't seem to notice.

"I don't think we have to take it that far. Let's just reserve the PDAs for Mr. Frederickson's benefit. If he's around, you can kiss me and I can kiss you."

"What about holding hands? Or putting your hand around my waist? I mean, there are ways to show affection that don't involve kissing." Her frustration had reached its tipping point. And it wasn't even related to the rules they were laying out. She was irritated that she wanted something she really shouldn't.

Isaac gave her a funny look. "As long as it's appropriate to do in front of my investor, then it's fair game. Does that work?"

Or I could just cuddle up to you whenever I feel like it. Like now.

"Sure." She pushed past him and headed for the door. If she had to spend another minute cornered by him, she didn't know if she'd be able to keep her real thoughts secret. It was like building a muscle. She needed to strengthen her ability to not react when he stared at her like that.

Chapter Thirteen

Isaac followed Olivia out into the hallway and down the stairs. Her pace was fast, making it hard to keep up with her. If they entered the dining room like this, the Fredericksons would assume they'd had a fight.

Which wasn't entirely untrue. They *had* argued.

But that wasn't the worst part.

He'd made a grave mistake. And the realization of that mistake was staring him in the face.

He never should have kissed her. He should have dropped the whole issue right from the start. Because now he wanted to pull her into his arms again and kiss her properly. Yes, that last kiss had been laced with spite. He'd wanted to prove a point, but the only point he'd driven home was to himself: she was a good kisser.

Better than good—she was the best he'd ever had and she hadn't even been trying.

Relationships weren't all about chemistry, though. If he needed to repeat that statement a hundred times over, he would. Olivia wasn't his type . . . even if she did create a fire that refused to die within him. His whole body had woken up.

He let out a growl, shoving down the betraying thoughts. If he couldn't get a handle on these emotions, then this week wasn't going to turn out the way he wanted at all.

Isaac sprinted forward a few steps and not a moment too soon. The second before she entered the dining hall, he was able to slip his hand into hers, lacing their fingers together. A spark of electricity shot from her hand to his and it took everything in his power not to pull away and stare at the strange occurrence.

Olivia's eyes dropped to where he held her hand and her jaw tightened. At least she didn't pull away. And now she was forced to walk a little slower. They entered the dining room and it felt like they'd been transported back in time to when St. Nicholas was a real person. The long mahogany table was adorned with all kinds of Christmas-themed décor from pine boughs to holly, to candles. There was a seven-foot Christmas tree in the corner decorated with silver and red ornaments. The red tablecloth that sat beneath the décor was a stark contrast to the white tableware.

Olivia sucked in a breath and her eyes widened.

"Do you like it?" Mr. Frederickson seemed to materialize from out of nowhere. "My wife fancies herself a decorator for this holiday." He chuckled and gestured toward a woman who entered from another doorway.

Mrs Frederickson was sweet-faced, white-haired, and as rounded as her husband. She carried a tray with a large Hawaiian pizza on it and smiled warmly at them.

"Christmas is my absolute favorite holiday. And since my children are all grown up and in other parts of the country, I fully intend to enjoy my traditions with our guests. I'm Lucille and I insist you call me that. None of this Mrs. Frederickson business in our home."

Isaac glanced at the table where there were only four place settings. "How many people are you expecting?"

"Oh, you're the first to arrive. There will be more over the next few days, but the biggest event will be the party on Friday. We hold an auction every year and use all the proceeds to deliver presents from Santa to local women's shelters."

"That's amazing." Olivia stepped forward but he held her hand tightly, unwilling to lose the connection they currently shared. She glanced at him with what felt like annoyance, but then it could have been much worse than that. He smiled at her, relishing the way he affected her. She tugged on him, her hand still in his, before she turned back to Lucille. "I used to volunteer for things like that when I was a teenager. We'd pick secret Santa names at the mall from a tree. Sometimes we'd help deliver the gifts. I still try to find needy families around the holidays when I can."

All eyes were on Olivia, and Isaac couldn't help but be in awe of her. Based on where she lived and the state of her apartment, he couldn't imagine that she had much to give. And yet she was so selfless that she insisted on sharing her goodwill with others.

Something caught in his throat. And tugged at his heart.

She briefly met his gaze, then looked away. All he could do was squeeze her hand, but when he did, she pulled her hand from his and clasped it with her other one.

"It's wonderful to see that the younger crowd still cares about charitable projects." Mr. Frederickson winked. "It looks like you two are peas in a pod."

Isaac smiled tightly and shot a glance in Olivia's direction. He wouldn't expect her to know about his charitable contributions, but then why would she? It wasn't something he actively boasted. It defeated the purpose, in his opinion.

Mr. Frederickson gestured toward the chairs. "Take a seat and we can dig in. We have pizza, breadsticks and some pasta."

"It looks delicious." Olivia moved toward a chair and he lurched forward to pull it out for her. She eyed him as if she were suspicious about his intentions. He couldn't blame her. He was almost a stranger to her.

He took a seat beside her, earning himself a side-eyed glance. Isaac knew he wasn't the best at reading her, but he could tell she hadn't let down her walls again. She sat stiffly, filling her plate and listening to the conversation. He needed to figure out a way to call a truce. That was the only option at this point.

After that kiss, he knew he couldn't leave things the way they were. He actually cared what she thought about him—a realization that hit him harder than he'd expected. Isaac served himself some pasta and breadsticks, racking his mind for what he could do to make it up to her. He'd already apologized. What more was there?

If he were dealing with someone he'd done business with, he'd win back their trust over time with several small acts. He'd bend over backward to show them that he wanted their business.

"Tell me, Olivia. How did you and Isaac meet?" Lucille asked.

His head snapped up. Uh oh. He'd been so focused on learning little things about her and making sure she knew about him that they hadn't discussed how they'd met.

"It's actually a funny story."

It was? Isaac's eyes cut to Olivia.

This doesn't sound good.

He didn't know Olivia intimately, but one thing he did know was that her sense of humor wasn't the same as his, and in all likelihood wasn't the same as the two people sitting across from them.

"I'd love to hear it." Lucille wiped her mouth, then placed her napkin on the table. "Samuel and I met when I was attending Cornell University. We bumped into one another at the library and he pretended to be lost." She offered her husband a smile and he reached for her hand, bringing it to his lips.

"I was smitten the moment I saw her."

They turned their attention to Olivia and Lucille beamed. "Go on. Tell us your story."

Olivia didn't miss a beat. "The first time we met was at a coffee shop."

Not that.

He reached for her hand, praying she'd tread carefully, but she dodged him and picked up a breadstick to place on her plate next to one she hadn't even taken a bite out of.

"We literally bumped into each other because this one wasn't looking where he was going. I then had to go to work smelling like a cup of coffee. The one he spilled all over me."

Their hosts shifted their attention to him and he squirmed in his seat.

"That's because I was so blinded by your beauty I had a momentary lapse in my cognitive ability."

Olivia let out a little laugh. "Oh, don't sugarcoat it, honey." She turned toward the older couple and leaned forward over the table, her conspiratorial tone drawing them in. "We couldn't stand each other when we first met."

Great. This wasn't how their first evening was supposed to go. He slumped back in his seat, ready to succumb to whatever plan she had for him. Hopefully she wouldn't take this fake relationship so far off the rails that his investor decided to walk away.

Olivia's smile widened. "I have to give you a little fore-warning; I can be a bit of a spitfire when the situation calls for it. So the next time I saw Isaac, I poured my iced coffee on him."

He shut his eyes tight. She wasn't even glamorizing the story one bit. Why couldn't she make it sound a little bit romantic? He didn't dare to look in Mr. Frederickson's direction for fear he would see horrified disgust in his face. He probably thought Olivia was too much of a wild card.

Everything was blowing up in his face. He should have known better than to involve a woman like Olivia.

The room was quiet.

Too quiet.

Just when he thought he'd need to jump in and explain that Olivia was making it sound worse than it was, the room erupted in laughter.

His eyes flew open and shot toward the Fredericksons, their faces full of humor.

"That sure sounds like the beginnings of an interesting relationship. You two must have quite a love story for you to be together after such a tumultuous start." Lucille set a smile on him that made him want to reconsider everything he knew about wooing his clients. He glanced at Olivia, who was conveniently looking anywhere but at him.

She took a sip of her beverage and shot a look in his direction. She didn't look the least bit guilty. She did, however, appear more relaxed—as if she was able to let out some steam from their previous argument. Maybe that was just how things worked with her. She wanted to feel in control.

Well, her desire to be in control wasn't something that could be appeased the whole time they were here. But if it managed to smooth some of her rough edges for now, he'd allow it. Then again, maybe he was allowing it for deeper reasons. Their kiss came to mind, among other things. Her fingers laced in his. The zap of electricity every time they touched. The twitch of her mouth when she was holding in a laugh.

If this situation were different, perhaps their relationship *could* work. Was that something he wanted? He'd told Bart he didn't have time for such frivolous ventures. But Olivia seemed to have risen above his expectations.

He stared at her thoughtfully, having no trouble finding the words to agree with Lucille. "Words don't do Olivia justice. Just when you think you've got her figured out, she ends up surprising you. That's what made me fall in love with her."

Lucille crooned, but Isaac's focus wasn't on his investor's wife. It was on Olivia. Everything he'd just said was weighted heavily with truth. He'd been so closed off from the world, so focused on what he thought he wanted; it had taken meeting someone who turned his world upside down to make him realize he was missing a heck of a lot in his life.

No, he wasn't in love. He knew that much.

But Olivia was something that intrigued him, made him want to get to know her better.

She shifted in her seat and offered a strained smile to their hosts. They had no reason to read her discomfort, and the signs were miniscule. But he could see it in the way she worried the napkin between her fingers in her lap. He'd disrupted the ecology of her personality.

For once he'd surprised her, and he was darn pleased with himself for having done so.

Isaac reached for her hand, still feeling the Fredericksons's eyes on them. Olivia resisted at first, but slowly released her napkin and allowed him to brush a kiss across her knuckles. Her eyes locked with his—only momentarily —then she sucked in a short gasp and pushed her chair out with a screech.

"I'm terribly sorry, but it's been a long day and I need to use the restroom."

Lucille rose and nodded to a young woman who had apparently been standing near the door this whole time. "Violet, will you see to it that Olivia finds the closest restroom?"

Olivia scrambled from her chair, her knee colliding with the wooden frame. She winced, shot Isaac a look that was so brief he couldn't read it, then hurried from the room.

He stared after her, wondering if it would be a good idea to follow her and make sure she was all right. But he thought better of it. With his hosts still in the room watching him, it would be best to continue being the gracious guest. Isaac smiled brightly. "What's on the schedule tomorrow?"

Chapter Fourteen

Olivia's knee throbbed. She hadn't thought she'd hit it that hard, but with each excruciating step, it continued to scream at her in protest. She was just thrown off balance. A hot bath would fix her right up.

Well, part of me.

Her heart was racing in circles in her chest, bouncing against her ribcage. She'd come to dinner fully intent on getting him out of her head. He wasn't Prince Charming. But no matter how many times she repeated that phrase in her head, he kept doing and saying things that could prove her wrong and it infuriated her.

From the moment he'd kissed her, she hated herself for how her body had reacted. Her head was the only part of her that was thinking clearly. She needed to stay on her A-game if she wanted to keep him at arm's length.

But then he would look at her with those eyes that made her insides melt like the gooey cheese in a toasted sandwich. It wasn't fair. No matter how many ideas she came up with to irritate him, it wasn't working.

And then he had to go and say something sweeter than

any of her real boyfriends had ever said—contributing to the chaotic thumping of her heart.

Violet gestured toward a door and smiled sweetly. "I can wait for you if you'd—"

"No, I'm sure I can find my own way back. Thank you."

The woman looked to be as old as her mother and was probably the housekeeper or some other servant that only the wealthy people could hire. She wondered if Isaac had someone like that on his staff.

She waited for Violet to disappear around a corner, then Olivia took off down another hallway that appeared to lead outside. She wanted fresh air, and the frigid cold of a New York December might just be the shock her body needed to get her head on straight. Isaac was a jerk and a liar who wasn't good for her. He was definitely *not* her type and she couldn't let that fact get covered up by her romantic nature.

She made it to a pair of double doors and slipped outside before she got caught. Carefully closing the door behind her, she leaned against it, her head thumping against the glass pane. Her eyes closed and she allowed herself to succumb to the calming scent of fresh pine from a large wreath that hung overhead. The cold air nipped at her nose and cheeks, and the wind whistled through the bare branches of trees nearby.

She wasn't some lovesick young woman whose only desire in life was to find a man to marry and take care of her. She was a strong independent woman with a firm grasp of who she was. She loved her job. There was nothing else she wanted in her life besides stability, and money could offer that. Did she want to move up at Maple Gardens? Sure. Was she willing to work hard to do that? Of course.

Her stomach clenched and chills traveled up her spine.

Subconsciously, she rubbed at the spot on her hand where he'd kissed it. With one look, he'd been able to shatter everything she thought of him. With one phrase she found herself wishing this trip had more truth in its foundation than it did. And she still couldn't figure out where everything had changed. Was she so shallow that one kiss was all it took to make her swoon? Because she certainly didn't believe in fairytales. True love's first kiss was a story mothers told their daughters a long time ago to get them married off and out of the house.

Olivia slid down the door and sat on the concrete, finally opening her eyes, though she couldn't see much in the dark. The moon was covered by clouds drifting by. It appeared she was in the backyard—no roads or driveways. This house had to be incredibly old to have such large gardens in this part of town. At least the Fredericksons were nice. She didn't get the feeling she had to impress them as much as Isaac had let on. It should be simple enough to play the role she'd been hired for, even if the thought made her stomach churn.

She vaguely registered the sound of the latch as someone turned the knob before the door swung inward. With her support suddenly gone, Olivia fell onto her back, not hard enough to hurt anything other than her pride. Isaac stared down at her.

Olivia expected him to be upset. She'd ditched dinner and left him to fend for himself without his partner in crime. Instead, he wore a crooked grin. "I abhor being the third wheel. Do you often disappear without a moment's notice? If so, tell me now." He offered his hand to her, helping her to her feet. But her knee gave way and she stumbled into him.

His arms wrapped around her waist and their gazes

locked. Every preconceived notion she had about him was quickly crumbling. It was like the more time she spent with him, the more he was willing to show her.

Was it really all that surprising? People like Isaac and Bart had a tendency to hold their cards close to their chests. They had to. There were so many people out in the world wanting to take advantage of them.

She'd never been one to let her first impressions dictate how she viewed someone long-term—until she'd met Isaac. What was it about him that made her want to push him away and draw him closer at the same time?

Her head spun. Blinking, she attempted to step away from him, assuming his closeness was the cause of her disorientation. Isaac refused to release her.

"Are you okay?" His warm breath fanned against her still cool cheeks, causing fresh chills to attack her body from the inside out.

Olivia shivered and shook her head. Then she nodded. "I'm fine. I just—"

"No, you're not. I'm sure you're exhausted. Call it jet lag or stress from our current. . . situation—either way, you should get some rest."

She nodded, not willing to argue as her dizziness came and went. "You're probably right." But before she could take a step, he scooped her into his arms. Her eyes flew wide and she let out a soft yelp. "What are you doing?"

"I'm taking you to our room. You're in no condition—"

"I can still walk, you—"

"Is everything all right?" Lucille materialized in the hallway with Violet by her side. "Did something happen?" Concern etched her features.

Isaac adjusted Olivia in his arms. "She'll be fine. Just

111

had a long day." He winked at the woman. "And perhaps a little overtired."

Relief relaxed Lucille's features. "Get some rest, dear. We'll be going on a sleigh ride tomorrow and would love you along, if you're up to it."

They moved past their host and her housekeeper and toward the stairs. Isaac wasn't even breathing heavily as he walked. His focus was set on the path before them. He probably wasn't going to talk to her because someone might overhear. And if he didn't want anyone to hear what he might say, then she'd keep her mouth shut as well.

She didn't know when it happened, but by the time they got to their room, she'd melted into him, curled up like a child. It wasn't because she enjoyed being close to him.

No.

She had been cold and taken off guard, that was all.

Isaac pushed open the door and moved swiftly through the room. He deposited her on the bed and immediately dropped down onto his knee to remove her boots.

Olivia yanked her foot away from him. "You don't have to do that."

He gave her a funny kind of grin, one that made all of those strange feelings float to the surface again. "I've realized that I haven't been treating you the way you deserve."

Her brows shot up. What? She had to be hearing things. Or maybe *he* was going crazy. "Did your investor put you up to this? Did he catch on that we're not really a couple?"

Isaac frowned. "What? Of course not. Why would you even ask that?"

"Because you carried me to our room. Now, you're helping me with my boots. Quite honestly, you're doing everything a boyfriend is supposed to do but you're not my boyfriend. Not even close."

She hadn't meant for her words to sound harsh, but the way he flinched had her second-guessing herself. Wait a minute. Had she misjudged even the strange situation they found themselves in?

Ohhh. He was method acting. He was getting into the zone so he could show off. That's what it was.

Olivia used the tip of her toe to push him away. "I can handle getting ready for bed all on my own, thank you."

He fell back onto his behind and stared up at her, the amusement in his gaze still apparent. What was wrong with this guy?

Furthermore, what was wrong with her that she allowed herself to be affected by that smile and the way his eyes locked with hers?

"Stop it."

His brows lifted. "I didn't do anything."

"You know very well what you're doing. And I don't approve. So just stop it. Right now." She gripped her boot with both hands and tossed it onto the floor. Then she did the same thing with the other, avoiding his stare.

"I seriously have no idea what you're talking about."

She could hear the smile in his voice and knew if she looked over at him she would definitely regret it. Olivia got to her feet and hobbled over to her suitcase. She found a pair of pajamas and edged toward the bathroom. "I'm taking a shower."

"Why are you limping—"

The second Olivia was in the bathroom, she swiftly shut the door and leaned against it as if that would be enough to separate her from the man in the other room. Now, if she could only barricade her heart.

Though that seemed less likely. The little traitor beating in her chest seemed insistent on pointing out all of Isaac's good qualities—things that made him marriage material. What was even more absurd was the fact that she was *not* looking for a long-term relationship and definitely not one with the likes of Isaac Spencer.

But he was smart, handsome, generous, and good to his mother. There were worse things than finding a guy who had to fib a little to get an investor to take his business seriously.

What was she thinking? Honesty was a top priority when finding someone to marry.

Olivia let out a frustrated groan and threw her pajamas on the floor by the door before turning on the water. A fine waterfall of warm water enticed her straight in and she let it run over her head. Instead of opening her eyes to find the shampoo she managed to knock the open bottle onto the floor, the contents spilling where it landed. When she reached down for it, her sore knee gave way and her foot hit the puddle with just the right amount of force, sending her feet in the air and her rump to the floor.

The pain from her fall was nothing compared to the terror she felt when the bathroom door swung open.

Chapter Fifteen

Isaac held his hand over his eyes as he stood in the doorway. "Olivia? Are you okay? What happened?"

"Get out!" she shrieked. "Don't you know how to knock?" She let out a sound that resembled a groan of exasperation mingled with pain.

His heart pounded. The second he'd heard the crash he'd reacted. People died from slipping in showers. All they had to do was hit their head on something with just the right angle and they were toast. "Answer the question," he demanded, still covering his eyes.

"What?" She demanded. "I said get out!"

"I'm not leaving unless I know you're okay. You might have a concussion."

"If I could be so lucky."

"What?"

She groaned again. "Then I wouldn't have to remember a single thing that happened today."

A smile played on his lips. "I don't think that's how it works."

"Will you just go now?"

"Are you all right?"

He could hear some shuffling even through the sound of the running water. "I think I twisted something." The room went quiet except for the sound of the shower. Then she let out a sharp cry. His whole body stiffened, and he moved farther into the bathroom.

"What on earth do you think you're doing?"

He froze. "It sounds like you need help."

"Not naked I don't. You shouldn't even be in here."

Isaac turned around, his back to the shower. His focus swept through the bathroom until he found a stack of towels on a shelf. He grabbed one and tossed it behind him toward her.

Olivia gasped.

"Wrap it around yourself so I can check that you're okay."

"Over my dead body."

"I promise to be a complete gentleman."

"A gentleman wouldn't be in here in the first place."

His patience was wearing thin. "Why are you being so stubborn? Just put on the stupid towel so I can help you."

The shower turned off. "Fine, you can help me out."

Isaac faced her, taking great care to avert his gaze so she didn't feel like he was gawking at her. "Do you think you can put any weight on it?" Awkwardly, he helped her to her feet by grasping her upper arms and lifting her from her fallen position. He slipped his arm around her waist and draped her arm over his shoulder.

Olivia put her foot down and winced. "I bumped my knee earlier. It will be fine."

He helped her limp toward the door and into the bedroom. Once he had her settled on the bed he gingerly touched the knee she favored. It looked a bit red and swollen. She grimaced a few times but other than that she didn't make a sound. This headstrong woman was more fiery and unpredictable than he could have ever imagined. But she was also strong and compassionate. The combination was as rare as they came. "I can let the Fredericksons know that you might need to head back sooner than expected."

Her features pinched and she set a scowl on him. "Don't you dare."

Was she suggesting that she actually wanted to stay with him despite having the perfect excuse to leave? Perhaps she was enjoying herself more than he realized.

"I didn't come all the way out here to just walk away when things get tough. You need your investor and I need my raise."

Oh. So that's where your heart is.

She didn't want to stay for him. She wanted to stay for her own needs. He couldn't blame her. That's how he had run his business for years. What was in the best interest of his board members? How could he guarantee he made the money he projected?

"May I remind you that your raise is based on your work ethic. If you have to leave early, that would be fine. Mr. Frederickson has met you. He believes that there is someone special in my life. If you want to leave, then leave."

She frowned, her eyes darting away as if she were unable to continue meeting his gaze.

And in that moment he realized his mistake. If she left, then he wouldn't have her company. In such a short amount of time, he'd grown accustomed to it. Dang it all! He didn't want her to leave.

Maybe he was just as selfish as everyone said he was.

Well, the option was out there. She had the choice to take it if she wanted. And he couldn't tell her not to.

"I'll get some ice for your knee."

It only took him a few minutes to find the kitchen. By the time he returned to the bedroom with an ice pack, Olivia had changed into her night clothes and was sitting on the side of the bed.

"Elevate the knee and keep this on it." Isaac turned on his heel and strode toward the bathroom. "I'm going to take my shower now. You have the bed."

"But where are you going to sleep?" Her voice was meek, almost timid. When he brought his gaze back to her, he found her staring at the ice pack.

"I'll sleep on the floor." He didn't give her a chance to look up at him before he headed for the bathroom once more. Everything had changed in an instant. He'd gone from merely tolerating her to wanting to spend more time with her and it had only been one day. The weeks they'd spent preparing for this trip hadn't managed to do that.

There has to be something in the air.

His shower was brief, but by the time he came out of the bathroom in just a pair of sweatpants, she was under the covers. Her back was turned toward the door and, from the looks of it, her breathing was slow and steady. He stood in the doorway, letting the light behind him spill into the room just enough for him to put together a bed. If he was lucky, there would be additional linens in the closet. There was no way he would be willing to explain why he needed the bedding. The Fredericksons had already assumed his relationship with Olivia was far more intimate.

He ran a hand through his damp hair and let out another sigh. Whatever Olivia chose in the morning, he'd have to be supportive. It wasn't like he could take back his offer. How would that go over?

Hey Olivia, I spoke too soon. I need you to stay. Not because of Mr. Frederickson, but because I find you captivating.

He could already see Olivia's reaction. She'd laugh at him and call him ridiculous. She'd point out that they couldn't be more different and he needed to shut his feelings down on the matter. And she'd be right. He couldn't just switch things on her like that so suddenly.

But maybe he could continue whittling away at her defenses until she was willing to give him a chance. If she stayed, this would be the perfect opportunity to get to know the woman behind the mask.

The thumping in his chest eased up a little then started right back up. The erratic pacing couldn't possibly be healthy. He needed to find his happy place. And whether or not that included Olivia would ultimately be decided in the morning.

Isaac stretched his arms out over his head and opened his eyes, wincing as the light from the nearby window hit him square in the face. He'd opted to sleep on the chaise lounge, but his feet had dangled off the edge, chilling him the entire night. To say that he'd slept restlessly was an understatement.

His focus shifted toward the bed and he froze. Olivia was still in bed but sitting up with the covers pulled up around her shoulders. Isaac sat upright. "How did you sleep?"

Her hands traced over the comforter and she offered him a small smile as she glanced at him out of the corner of her eye. "This bed is amazing. It's ten times better than the one I have at home." Her gaze moved to the chaise and her pretty smile went lopsided. "I can't imagine you can say the same."

He stretched again then tilted his head side to side until he'd adjusted his neck properly. "You'd be right."

The room turned quiet. He waited for her to tell him her ultimate decision. She might have been waiting for him to say his own piece, but he had nothing left. The waiting was agony and he refused to show any more of his cards to this woman who had managed to throw him so far off guard he was in another state.

Finally, she cleared her throat and tucked her hair behind her ear before setting him with a firm stare. "I've thought about what you said last night—about me leaving."

"Yeah?"

She nodded. "And I think you're wrong."

He sat a little taller. "Pardon me?"

Olivia looked away and shifted in her seat again. "I think you're wrong that Mr. Frederickson would be okay with me leaving so soon after getting here. I'm sure we can figure out a way to make this trip still work even if my knee is a bit uncomfortable."

He didn't know if he was more terrified or thrilled. Olivia wasn't going home. He had a chance to win her over. All he had to do was prove he was the man she needed him to be.

Easier said than done.

"Do you think you can walk today?"

"It's still tender. But much better than last night." Olivia lifted her eyes to meet his. "We're doing the sleigh ride today?"

He nodded.

"Maybe if I ice it a little more?"

"I don't want you to overdo it."

She sliced her hand through the air with a dismissive motion. "I've had worse. I'm sure I'll be fine."

He couldn't imagine what worse meant to her but one thing he did know was that Olivia needed looking after. And he'd make sure she didn't regret her decision to stay.

Chapter Sixteen

Olivia sat on the bed wrapped in one of the dressing gowns she'd found hanging in the robe, her thoughts swirling.

Warmth twirled deliciously inside her, filling her stomach, her lungs, and her heart with a strange sense of wonder. Isaac had gone to find breakfast for her and insisted she rest as long as she wanted.

Granted, he'd made a good point about their hosts looking down on anything less than him acting like a doting boyfriend. But there were several routes he could have taken to avoid their judgment.

He could have gone to breakfast and told them she didn't feel well and sent up the housekeeper to tend to her. Wasn't that the sort of thing that happened in all the movies?

That's definitely what happened in the Austen-era books she'd loved reading in high school.

She nibbled on her lower lip, biting into the tender flesh, attempting to fight the silly little grin she could feel spreading across her face. Isaac wasn't so bad. Her stomach did its own belly flop, and she wrapped her arms around her middle to quell the motion inside. Isaac might be pretending they're a couple, but she knew better than to believe that he could fake all of it. Not even Isaac was *that* great of an actor.

Olivia shifted to the edge of the bed when the door swung open with a bang. She gasped and her head whirled around to find Isaac balancing an oversized tray with both hands. His head snapped up and he gave her a surprised look.

"That door felt heavier when I left. Do you think they heard me kick it?"

She covered her mouth, stifling a giggle. "I think even the neighbors down the street heard it."

"It wasn't that bad." He rolled his eyes and smirked at her, then shifted, hooking his foot around the door and closing it gently. "I guess we'll figure it out soon enough. If anyone comes up to investigate, let's tell them it was you."

Olivia grinned then covered her mouth again as the blush crept up her chest and into her face. She hadn't thought it was possible for Isaac to let his guard down like this. It was refreshing to say the least. "You're almost acting like a real person," she giggled. "I'll have to tell the girls you're not a robot after all."

He froze . . . and that's when she realized she'd said that out loud.

One of his brows lifted. The expression on his face was the same judgmental one he'd used with her at the beginning.

Her eyes rounded to the size of teacup saucers and she clamped both hands over her mouth. "I'm sorry. I didn't mean—" She watched in absolute shock as he tossed his head back and laughed.

"Is that what they're calling me these days?"

She blinked. A few times.

Isaac shook his head and strode across the floor.

"You're not . . . mad?"

He peeked at her as he placed the tray on the bed and shifted to sit with it between them. "That people at Maple Gardens think I'm a robot? Nah. I've heard worse. You seem to forget that my mother lives there. I've heard it all. But 'robot' . . ." He picked up a piece of toast and pointed the corner at her before tearing off a bite. ". . . *that* one's new." He seemed more thoughtful than upset as he chewed. "I think Bosshole was the worst one by far."

Her mouth fell open for the second time that morning. "No one has called you that at Maple Gardens."

He shook his head. "No, that one is reserved for the people at the corporate offices." He gave her a comedic grimace. "I guess I'm a little hard on some of my employees. There are just certain things I can't afford for them to get wrong. When I call them out on it, I end up getting the fun nicknames. Though, come to think of it, I haven't heard that particular gem for a few years now." His smile made her heart melt, gooey and dripping all over her insides. "I guess I'm mellowing out a little."

She cleared her throat and shifted her focus to the food on the tray. She didn't know if he was mellowing or if she was just starting to realize he wasn't as bad as she thought he was. She reached for a strawberry and popped it in her mouth. "Were the Fredericksons upset that we're missing breakfast with them?"

"Not at all. They were worried about you though. They insisted on sending their masseuse up after breakfast to take a look at you."

Her eyes cut to him but before she could argue he

chuckled and held up his hand. "Don't worry, I told them they didn't need to."

She relaxed. "You did?" Was she so easy to read? Had he figured her out that quickly?

"Of course. Based on the way you've been acting like a stray cat who doesn't want anyone to bring it home—"

She shot a dark look in his direction which only deepened the amusement in his expression.

"I figured you'd rather not be given too much attention over the matter."

"Thank you," she murmured with relief.

"Perhaps you can explain it to me though."

Olivia picked up a grape and tossed it in her mouth and the tart juices splattered in her mouth when her teeth bit down on the delicate fruit. "Explain what?"

"Why are you so insistent that people don't take care of you?"

Her friend Izzie came to mind. They'd had a similar conversation once. Izzie hated that Bart wanted to buy her things thanks to a lot of childhood baggage. But he'd been patient, showing his love the way he knew best, and over time Izzie had relaxed her stance.

I told her she needed to take care of herself and that included letting love in.

Olivia's eyes darted to Isaac and then back to the tray of food as she squirmed under his gaze. This was different. There was no "showing his love" going on here. "I have nothing against someone taking care of me."

At his pointed look, she let out an exaggerated sigh. "I *do*, however, hate it when a stranger insists on doing something for me. There's always ulterior motives." She grimaced. Izzie had said something similar. But where her friend was wrong was clear. Bart loved her and his gifts were thoughtful. Isaac was a work colleague. More or less. If he wouldn't have helped her in some other context, then she didn't want his help now.

"What do you mean ulterior motives? Do you think that I would expect you to do something in return? You realize that's the definition of a quid pro quo, right? What about the Fredericksons? Do you think they are offering their private massage therapist because they expect their charity to be repaid?"

When he said it that way, she sounded just like Izzie had. Shaking her head, she brushed her fingers on her pants and glanced toward the window—anywhere but at Isaac's discerning gaze. "Obviously there are going to be exceptions. Generally speaking, I don't like taking charity. I've gotten this far in my life without anyone's help. I'm happy to keep it that way."

He was quiet for a moment before he spoke again. "I can appreciate that."

Chills raced up and down her skin. She had expected another argument. He was supposed to tell her she was wrong and she needed to show some humility when she needed it.

Instead, he'd listened. He acknowledged that her opinion on this matter was valid. Slowly, she lifted her focus to him. "You're not toying with me, are you?"

Isaac leaned back, his palms on the comforter behind him. He studied her with that same thoughtful expression from before. "No. I couldn't be more sincere. Now, do I agree? Absolutely not."

A small smile stole across her face. "I guess I should have realized that. But I refuse to depend on anyone for anything. People are the only constant—"

"Exactly, they're the only constant. So, you should be willing to allow yourself to let them in."

She shook her head. "Let me finish. People are the only constant in that they ultimately fail you."

His brows furrowed. "That's a little harsh, don't you think?"

Olivia gave him a sad smile. "You read through my background. My life doesn't have the stability you preach about. Exhibit A—my parents, whoever they were, didn't want me."

"What are you talking about? Your parents are in the Cayman Islands for the holidays."

It hurt her. Old wounds opening up out of the blue. This wasn't something she'd told anyone. Not even Izzie. Her friend had her own demons to deal with, she didn't need to worry about Olivia's, too.

"The woman who birthed me left me at a fire station when I was five. The parents you looked up were my foster parents. They raised me. But they refused to adopt me. I can't complain too much, at least they didn't ship me off to other foster homes. And before you ask, I guess there was just too much red tape when it came to making it official. My biological mom came into the picture a few times and the state wanted to wait and see if anything would come of it. Reunification and all that." She hated how her voice broke. Swallowing hard, she forced a smile, her eyes shining. "See? I have a thousand stories just like that one. But I'm strong. I got through it. That's what made me tough and I refuse to allow myself to lean on anyone who will inevitably fail me."

His brows were drawn together as if he couldn't quite get her words to sink in. "But your foster parents are still your parents. They're the ones you visit on the holidays. They're the ones who check in on you—"

"You're missing the point of this story. I know they love me. And yes, they've helped me over the years when I've really needed it. They're not strangers. But they also never fought for me like I wanted—like I needed them to. Look, I didn't want to turn this into a big ole pity party. I'm fine. Like I said, I'm a big girl and I can take care of myself. Are there situations when I'm forced out of my comfort zone? Sure. But usually, if I have a say, I prefer not asking for help." She leaned over and picked up a piece of toast. "So, how are we spending the rest of the day before we go on that sleigh ride?"

Despite her light tone, she could tell something didn't sit well with Isaac. His cheek twitched and his brows were still pinched.

"Earth to Isaac."

He started, then brought his eyes to meet hers. "What? Oh. They said we could decorate some cookies for the party if you're up for it. I guess you can frost a cookie just as easily sitting as you can standing."

"That sounds fun! When do we start?" She did her best to smile wide enough to put him at ease but only received a small offering from him.

"As soon as we're done eating."

"Great. I'll get dressed." She took a big bite of the toast as she slipped her legs from the bed.

I'll smile until my face hurts if it keeps everyone happy. I can do that.

Chapter Seventeen

Cookie in hand, Isaac glanced up at Olivia as she laughed with Lucille and frosted one of her own. Her eyes locked with his and something seemed to pass between them. He couldn't tell what it was exactly, but it wasn't at all unpleasant.

Olivia ducked her head, her smile still on her face.

"You two are *so* sweet, I can definitely tell you're in love," Lucille cooed. "I remember that feeling. The first time I saw Mr. Frederickson, I was utterly smitten." She glanced over to the table where her husband sat looking through some documents. "Of course, back then he'd actually decorate with me." She winked at Olivia and patted her hand. "You've got a good one. I can tell."

Olivia peeked at Isaac once more and that strange electrical current flowed between them again.

"Come on, Mr. Frederickson. Decorate cookies with your guests."

Mr. Frederickson shot a look in their direction. Isaac wasn't sure the man was going to give in, but then he tossed the folder on the table and crossed the room. "Didn't

I tell you family was important, son? There's nothing like finding your soul mate and spending the rest of your life with her by your side."

Isaac shifted, giving Mr. Frederickson ample space to be next to his wife. "I couldn't say it better myself," he murmured, once again meeting Olivia's eyes. Could she be that person for him?

So much about her had come to light this morning and he was still processing it. His initial judgment had been wrong. Yes, she was infuriatingly stubborn. And that mess of an apartment ruffled his preference for order, but there were layers to her that made him want to delve deeper and know more.

She was strong, independent, and yet she hadn't let her bad experiences turn her into something ugly. Nowadays, people used their past traumas as excuses for poor behavior.

But not Olivia.

"Oh, where are my manners? Isaac, you switch places with me so you can be next to your sweetheart."

He stilled, his eyes sweeping over to his investor's wife. She'd already moved toward him, not giving him the opportunity to decline her offer. She nudged him out of his spot, forcing him to walk around to the other side of the island where Olivia sat on a tall stool.

She looked at him from beneath her lashes and he couldn't help but stare. There was a smudge of powdered sugar on her cheek and he itched to wipe it away. His arm brushed against hers and Olivia glanced at him again. His stomach churned with disappointment. She very well could have been acting.

What was he thinking?

She *was* acting. That's what he'd hired her for.

His jaw tightened and he focused on the cookie in his hand, dismayed to find he'd held it a little too hard. What was supposed to be star-shaped was now a wonky triangle.

Olivia snickered and his eyes cut to hers.

"What?"

She shook her head and pressed her lips together—a snort still escaped. "Nothing."

This interchange seemed to have captured the attention of their hosts who looked on with amusement.

"What?" he repeated. "I'm not as skilled with a butter knife as some people."

Olivia laughed again and he smiled in response, loving the sound of it. She carefully retrieved the sad-looking sweet and handed him a bowl of sprinkles. "Maybe you should just do the finishing touches."

He scoffed. "I can frost. Look, I did that one." He pointed to a tree, then immediately regretted it. The frosting was uneven; thin in some places and falling off the side in others. He reached for the cookie, intent on fixing it, but she was too fast.

Olivia's hand snatched it and she grinned. "This one?"

He waited for her to laugh at him and point out all the mistakes he'd made. But instead, she examined it, turning it from side to side. He reached for it again. "Let me fix it—"

She held it just out of reach. "Why? It's perfect just the way it is." She put it down next to one of her perfectly painted ones and sprinkled a few green crystals on top. "Didn't you know? There's beauty in everything. Even lopsided cookies."

He was stunned. Who said stuff like that?

Angels, that's who.

Isaac got the sudden feeling that someone was staring at him.

131

Two someones.

He looked up to find the Fredericksons gazing at Olivia and himself. Lucille had a small smile on her face, as if she had expected Olivia to say the most perfect thing. Mr. Frederickson seemed almost as stunned—but in a good way. There was awe in his gaze. But then, Isaac was quickly realizing that it wasn't hard to admire a woman like Olivia. The more time he spent with her, the more that became clear.

There were no words to describe just how wonderfully different Olivia was.

The Fredericksons got called away shortly after that interaction. First, Mr. Frederickson had to answer a business call, much to Lucille's disappointment. But he offered to make it up to her. Then Lucille took her leave, needing to run a few errands.

This left Isaac alone with Olivia—something that both thrilled and terrified him. With their hosts gone, they only had the sound of soft Christmas music filling the void.

Olivia frosted a cookie and nudged it over to him; he pinched some sprinkles and spread them on top. The tension between them became intolerable—at least for him. It was hard to pin down what exactly made him uncomfortable. It could be the story she'd told him about her upbringing. Or it might be the fact that he continued to fight the feelings he was developing for her.

Regardless of the reasons, he needed to switch things up.

"Olivia?"

"Hmm?"

"Tell me about your Christmas traditions growing up."

Her hands stilled for a moment before she blinked and looked up at him. "What kinds of traditions did you want to know about?"

"You know. The usual. You're obviously very good at decorating cookies. I bet you did that a lot."

She put the cookie down and then the knife before facing him. "Is this about what I told you earlier? Are you trying to make me feel better about my family?"

His eyes widened and his heart stumbled. The knots in his stomach doubled then tripled and he felt the blood drain from his face. "What? No. I just—wanted to get to know you better, that's all."

Olivia tilted her head, pursing her lips as she studied him. "Okay. Fine. You want all the nitty gritty? I'll give it to you. Yes. Occasionally we decorated cookies. I got to open one present on Christmas Eve every year. Did I believe in Santa? That's a hard no. Did we do any of the other traditions? I guess we went caroling once." She smiled softly. "It was at one of those small towns where they really went all out decorating. It looked like a real magical Christmas village. You know, those tiny ones they set up in storefronts at Christmas time? But my most memorable Christmases weren't ones you'd want to hear about. So let's just pretend I had the perfect upbringing you believed me to have when you"—she used air quotes—"looked into my background."

Her tight tone had thrown him off and he edged closer. "Why didn't you believe in Santa?"

This time Olivia tossed her head back and let out a sharp laugh. "Seriously? What foster kid *did*? Sometimes people experience hardship that makes them smart. It's like I said—I couldn't count on anyone. Why would I put my faith in a being who was supposed to bring me my heart's desire when those around me couldn't even give me a family?" Her cheeks flushed and she looked away. It was clear she hadn't gotten past some of her childhood trauma.

Isaac felt the urge to wrap her up in his arms. And

before he could convince himself that was a *very* bad idea, he'd done just that.

His arms wrapped around her, pulling her against his chest.

She let out one small gasp of surprise, but didn't fight him. Instead, her arms came up under his arms and she clung to him. Olivia buried her face in his chest and her shoulders shuddered. Isaac rested his chin on top of her head, willing to hold her as long as she needed; as if doing so was the one thing that could help her work through this —which was ridiculous. He knew that.

Olivia was a grown woman. She had carried the extra baggage around for so long she probably forgot she had them. But who hadn't done the exact same thing these days? Heaven knew he had his own issues to work through. He'd been told by several people he was too scared to commit—it had nothing to do with liking his lifestyle the way it was.

She pulled back and let out a shy laugh, brushing briskly at her cheeks with her fingers. "I'm sorry. That was embarrassing."

He lifted her chin and studied her, waiting for her to meet his gaze. When her lashes finally lifted enough, he tipped his head. "Don't ever apologize for fighting off your demons. You're stronger than you know."

Her lashes fluttered again and her lips parted, drawing his attention. They were like rose-colored petals, soft and inviting. He'd kissed them before, tasted their sweetness, and it had nearly ruined him. Hadn't they agreed that kisses should be reserved for an audience? There was no one here to witness this demonstration. It would be wrong—*so wrong*—to steal a kiss, however brief. And yet he found himself inching, dipping closer.

Consequences? What consequences? Thoughts of anything that could possibly go wrong with such an advancement failed to breach the wall he'd drawn up in his mind. He needed to have her lips against his.

He was proving a hypothesis, he told himself. If their kiss failed to stir the same emotions as before, then he could blame it on hormones. But if their kiss jump-started the fire that fueled his very being, it would be all the proof he needed to finally push aside his preconceived notions against settling down.

Someone cleared their throat and Isaac jumped back, whirling to find Mr. Frederickson standing in the doorway. "My apologies for being gone so long. That phone call ran longer than I expected." He wore a knowing grin. "But don't stop on my account. I merely wanted to let you know that there has been a change of plans. Lucille and I must meet with a client of mine, so you two are welcome to take the sleigh ride on your own. Dinner will be served at a little cabin at the end of the trail. You two love birds enjoy yourselves." He grabbed the documents from the table and nodded once more before disappearing.

Isaac stood frozen, reality crashing down on him like a splash of cold water. He didn't know if he dared face her for fear she'd give him a lecture. The problem was, he needed to discuss this before it went too far and he got his heart broken.

Perhaps it was too late.

"I need to use the restroom," Olivia blurted. She scrambled from the stool and held up her hands before he could offer to help her. She hobbled out of the room and he had to stand there and watch like a helpless fool.

A fool in love.

Chapter Eighteen

Olivia splashed cold water on her face but it didn't seem to help her in the least. Her cheeks were still red, flushed from the desire that had started as a small flicker and quickly grew into a rolling fire.

She'd been frozen, helpless under his gaze.

Crazy. She was absolutely insane.

There was no other way to describe it. She'd allowed herself to want a guy who was so wrong for her. They couldn't be more different. She was a poor girl from the wrong side of the tracks, for heaven's sake.

Olivia braced herself on the counter, her fingers turning white as she clutched the edge with every last bit of strength she had.

Why did he have to be so sweet? Why couldn't he blow her off like all the other guys did? No one listened like he did. No one seemed to care how deep her scars were.

Which begged the question, why wasn't he dating anyone? Better yet why wasn't he married with three kids and a dog?

There had to be something wrong with him that she couldn't see.

Unless there wasn't.

She let out a groan and spun around to lean against the counter. This could be her chance at finding someone who could make her happy. She should just go for it. Even if he's only faking it for his investor—she could handle that. Right? It'd be nice to "date" someone decent for a change.

Pressing her palms to her flushed cheeks, Olivia let out a small laugh. What would Izzie think if she knew what was going on? She'd have a heyday with this one. Well, what she didn't know couldn't hurt her.

A soft knock at the door startled her enough she jumped.

"Olivia? You okay?" Isaac's quiet voice drifted through the door and Olivia's heart reacted just as it had when they'd nearly kissed.

She nodded then swallowed and squeaked, "Yes. I'm fine." Who was she kidding? She wouldn't be able to fake any of this. She just needed to figure out a way to tell him she was developing feelings for him.

Boy, that sounded stupid. But there was no other viable option.

Tonight when they went on their sleigh ride, she'd break the news. As far as she could tell, it would go one of two ways. She couldn't imagine him lying, but he might let her down easy. In that case they'd need to set up more ground rules—a thought that put her stomach on edge.

Then there was the more likely of the two options. Based on the way he was looking at her, it wasn't so far-fetched to believe he *might* share the same feelings.

Olivia dragged her hands through her hair and sighed.

The thought of having a conversation to define whatever this was absolutely terrified her.

Well, she'd never been one to shy away from something just because she was scared. She'd just have to squeeze her eyes shut and jump in with both feet.

———————

Olivia shuffled down the stairs toward the front door. Isaac had offered to help her, but she had outright refused. She needed a clear head if she was going to tell him what needed to be said.

Whether it was this place, or the holiday, she couldn't be certain. All she knew was that she had been looking for men in all the wrong places—or not at all—and now that she'd found one with potential, she couldn't let him slip through her fingers.

She turned the corner of the stairs and slowed, though her heart did the opposite. Gripping the railing with one hand to steady herself, she locked eyes with Isaac as he stood at the base of the stairway.

His adorable crooked grin was something she was quickly finding she loved. They both stood, frozen in time. All she wanted to do was memorize this moment—his eyes, his smile, and the way he looked at her.

Her. Olivia Todd.

Isaac was one of the most eligible bachelors of the state of Georgia and he was staring at her like she was literal royalty.

Every nerve in her body hummed with anticipation and she slowly made her way down the steps toward him. She needed to keep it together. She couldn't go flying off the handle and make him think she was crazy.

No.

Olivia would keep a clear head, tell him how she felt and promise herself that if he didn't return those feelings, she wouldn't go running to the nearest airport.

Okay, so that last bit wasn't a guarantee. She'd never actually initiated a "more than friends" conversation before. She wasn't sure she could handle rejection if he didn't reciprocate.

"Oh good! You're ready."

Warm blood that coursed through her body suddenly chilled. She paused on the second to last step as a new face entered the foyer. The man looked to be about ten years older than her. He was dressed for the outdoors and gestured toward something that was out of her view. A woman appeared around the corner and smiled warmly at her, though it didn't quell the anxiety that suddenly flooded Olivia's entire being. A quick glance in Isaac's direction confirmed he wasn't exactly thrilled. An entire conversation passed between them, but Olivia felt she'd missed the memo on how to decode it.

"Olivia, this is Mr. and Mrs. Tillie. They're friends of the Fredericksons who are here for the Christmas party." Isaac offered his hand to Olivia. "Mr. Tillie is interested in investing as well."

Olivia blinked and her eyes bounced to Mr. Tillie. "Well, I assure you that if you decide to do so, you won't be disappointed."

Tillie chuckled. "That's what Mr. Frederickson has said. I hope you don't mind us crashing your sleigh ride. Mr. Frederickson thought we wouldn't be up for any activities after arriving this afternoon, but we'll only be here for a short while, so we don't want to waste time resting. We'd love to take Mr. Frederickson and Lucille's place if that's okay."

Olivia swallowed down the bile that threatened to rise up her throat. Tonight had been meant to be just her and Isaac. She couldn't exactly tell him that she was falling for him in front of additional investors. Her stomach sank, though she prayed she hid it well with a smile she didn't feel like offering. "Of course you can come. The more the merrier."

The Tillies headed out the door before them and Olivia moved to follow, but Isaac held her back. He leaned close, his lips right behind her ear. "You okay?"

She jumped and stared at him. "Yes. Why do you ask?"

"You don't seem . . . I dunno . . . yourself."

Olivia let out a small, sharp laugh. "I'm fine. Looks like you're gonna have to be on your A-game though, if you want to double your investors."

His brows were creased and his jawline was rigid. The warmth in his gaze when he'd met her eyes as she headed down the stairs was all but gone.

She flicked him with the back of her fingertips. "Don't look so concerned. I'm here to be your wingman. Whatever you need, whatever game you want me to play, you just let me know." Even as the words escaped her lips, she felt sick to her stomach. This wasn't a game anymore—not to her. At least she didn't want it to be, but that was where it was, and it appeared that was where it would stay.

Olivia patted his cheek with her palm. "Come on, dear boyfriend," she drawled, "let's give them a show to remember."

His grip on her upper arm tightened, but not enough to cause her pain. His gaze drilled into her as he studied her.

Olivia shifted and offered a nervous laugh. "What? Is there something on my face?"

Isaac released her arm and shook his head. "No. You're perfect." He spun on his heel and strode toward the door.

Staring after him, her heart tripped over itself. She blinked a few times while trying to figure out what had just happened. Was he mad? Should she have told the Tillies that they were planning on this trip being a private getaway? That didn't make sense. The whole point for her being here was to win over as many investors as Isaac could get.

She sighed and slowly made her way toward the door.

If she knew one thing for certain, it was that Isaac Spencer had zero interest in her romantically. He might care about her wellbeing. And he depended on her to make this ruse of his work. But that was where his interest died.

Olivia sat beside Isaac, across from the Tillies. They shared a warm blanket over their laps and Isaac held her hand tightly in his.

Almost too tight.

The sleigh bounced across the ground as the horses pulled it along the snowbank. Bells jingled in the crisp evening air but did nothing to ease the tension Olivia felt dragging her down. Isaac was stiff beside her, his mannerisms no longer confident.

Maybe he didn't want these investors, though she couldn't tell why. They seemed nice enough.

Mrs. Tillie's smile might have been a little too big, but other than that they were perfectly normal.

"Lucille was able to tell me a little bit about you two

when I spoke to her on the phone this morning before our trip." Mrs. Tillie snuggled in closer to her husband. "Sounds like you two are still in that fresh state of love." She glanced up at Mr. Tillie with adoration. "If you're lucky, you'll always have it." When her eyes rested on Olivia again, she winked. "You know what I think? I think the two of you will always have it. I have a sense about these things."

If only this woman knew what was really going on, she'd eat her words. But now was not the time to mess things up. It was time to play her part.

Olivia grinned wide. "You are so sweet." She rested her head against Isaac's shoulder despite his stiff body being as fun to cuddle as a prickly cactus would be. "I knew I would love Isaac from the very first moment we touched." Was she imagining it, or was he leaning away from her?

He needed to get on board and fast.

She pulled back far enough to grasp his jaw with her fingers and force him to look at her while she still spoke to their guests. "There's just something about knowing you've found your better half, you know? Like God himself plucked that person and threw him right in your path because he knew you needed him more than breathing. More than life itself."

Chills assaulted her, ripping through her like the coldest wind at the top of the tallest mountain. All sights, sounds and smells faded into nothingness. She couldn't breathe, she couldn't speak as she stared into his eyes. Those eyes that flickered with a secret she could only dream of deciphering.

"That's so lovely. Are you a poet, perchance?"

Olivia dropped her hand and tore her eyes from his, breaking the spell he had on her. "No, actually. I'm just an admin assistant at a retirement center," she mumbled.

She shifted in her seat and released Isaac's hand. Her whole body shivered.

It was this dang cold weather she wasn't used to.

She didn't care if she was lying to herself. If that's what she had to do to get through tonight—to get through this week. She'd turn into Pinocchio if she had to.

Mrs. Tillie leaned forward and patted Olivia's knee. "Perhaps you should try. I'm not nearly as talented as you are, but I like to write down a few stanzas here and there when there are feelings my heart can't contain."

Olivia nodded and glanced out into the darkened woods. Maybe the woman had a point. It could be therapeutic to write down her feelings for Isaac.

Then burn the whole book.

Because having to relive these feelings over and over again wouldn't be healthy.

Not one bit.

Chapter Nineteen

The woman was utterly infuriating! One moment he could have sworn she was into him. Her gaze would lock onto his in such a way that made him feel like he was flying one second, but then it would shut down the very next.

Like today, for instance. While making cookies, she made him feel like he was unstoppable. Her affection was addictive and he wanted more. He had every intention of fleshing out whatever this was that continued to grow between them but then the Tillies had to arrive and throw everything off balance. Isaac could only pray that they would get the opportunity to have some alone time. Based on how interested the Tillies were, he didn't see much of a chance for that to happen. At the same time, he wasn't so sure spending one-on-one time with Olivia would be in his best interest. He couldn't get a read on her. The second she brought up that they were putting on a show, he'd just about lost it.

It took everything in his power not to drag her up to their room and demand that she have an adult conversation about where this was headed. The *only* thing that held him back was the fact that there was zero precedence for that. She would probably just laugh in his face and remind him that she was just his employee.

Every muscle in his body was tense. His heart and his head demanded closure. Even if it meant having his heart shredded in front of him and stomped into oblivion, he needed to know if there was a possibility they could make something work.

His jaw still tingled where she'd held it. His gut churned with the expectation of something more. And his ridiculous heart pleaded for him to do something to keep it beating.

The sleigh lurched to a stop as they came upon a cute little cabin covered in Christmas lights. There were lights lining the path leading to the front door. The whole place looked like a life-size version of a gingerbread house.

Isaac grasped Olivia's hand. Out of the corner of his eye, he noted her attention shifting to him but she didn't pull away.

For that, he could be grateful.

The Tillies climbed down first and then Isaac jumped down before lifting his hands up to Olivia. Once again, they held one another's gaze. A thousand conversations could have passed in those few seconds when she placed her hands on his shoulders and he held her waist.

He was vaguely aware of their guests disappearing inside when he placed Olivia on her feet. She didn't release him nor did he her.

Now.

He should tell her now—everything that was in his heart—before he lost the chance to do so again. Another opportunity might not present itself. "Olivia—"

"You two have to see this!"

Olivia turned, and the moment was lost. His heart

crumpled, defeated. Maybe he wasn't meant to tell her. Maybe that would just complicate things for the remainder of the week. Who was he kidding? If she told him she wasn't interested, it would definitely complicate things.

Her hands slipped from his neck and she nodded toward the cabin. "Shall we?" She offered her hand and he accepted. This was all part of the plan, was it not? Win over his investors. Play pretend. Don't get attached.

Well, he was failing miserably with at least two of those.

"So, Mr. Spencer. Mind if I ask you a personal question?"

Isaac groaned inwardly. Mrs. Tillie wouldn't let up. She was nice and all, but she couldn't take a hint. After they were done eating, she insisted they sit in the living room by the fireplace and get to know everyone better.

Her husband didn't seem to mind, but all Isaac wanted was to spend some time alone with Olivia.

Instead, he smiled at Mrs. Tillie and nodded. "Go for it. I'm an open book."

Olivia rested, curled up in a ball beside him, her head in his lap. Her eyes were closed but he could tell she was on edge. Today had taken a toll on her and he couldn't blame her. He played with the ends of her hair, marveling at the soft curls within his fingertips.

"Why haven't you gotten married before now?"

His head shot up and he tensed. "Pardon?"

"Leave the boy alone. He was obviously waiting for the right woman." Mr. Tillie winked at Isaac.

Olivia didn't stir, but there was no way she wasn't asleep.

Isaac cleared his throat then attempted to swallow the lump that had lodged there. "Right," he wheezed. "I was waiting for the right girl."

Mrs. Tillie clicked her tongue. "No. A handsome boy like you?" Her eyes dropped to Olivia and she lowered her voice. "I can appreciate waiting for someone special, I am a romantic after all. But usually a man in your position at least *attempts* to settle down. There are so many who divorce these days."

Mr. Tillie shifted in his seat. "I have to admit, when I heard about you and the business you were in, I had assumed you would have started a family by now. It shows stability. A man with a family doesn't make poor business decisions. He has mouths to feed."

Isaac turned his focus back to Olivia's hair. He could lie, say he was looking for someone special—waiting for the love of his life. But people like the Tillies could probably see right through him. "Honestly, I didn't want to get married . . . before now."

Despite the roaring fire and the warmth of Olivia in his lap, the room seemed to get colder by a few degrees.

Isaac lifted his gaze to the couple in front of him. "My father left my mother when I was a teenager. Ran off with a woman who worked for him. I didn't see the point in getting married when a promise that important could be broken so easily by either party." His voice cracked and emotion burned behind his eyes. His mother had dealt with it a lot better than he had. They didn't talk much about it. In fact, at the time she'd acted like his dad didn't exist. Like she'd never been married. It had gotten to the point where he wasn't sure it had. The memories had been buried so deep that they almost didn't exist at all. Isaac hadn't told anyone that story. Not even Bart. All his friend knew was that he didn't want to settle down and start a family. And now those memories were being dredged up, only it didn't hurt as much as he had expected.

In fact, it didn't hurt at all.

He gazed down at Olivia, a small smile touching his lips as she continued to pretend to be asleep . . . and then the realization hit him. She was the first woman he had ever met who had changed his mind on the matter.

That was also why his heart was so invested in finding out if she felt the same.

Lifting his focus to the Tillies, he waited for his story to sink in before speaking again. "To me, marriage means total commitment. I treat my businesses the same way. Everything I put my heart into, I do it one hundred and ten percent. Everything I have, I owe to my instincts and hard word. I don't believe in luck."

He dropped his attention to the beauty before him.

Well, maybe luck played a small part in his life. He just had to find out.

Isaac paced outside of the bathroom door like a lunatic. The Tillies had remained glued to their side for their entire outing. They even insisted on walking up the stairs together. He and Olivia finally got a tiny bit of peace when their door shut.

But the second he turned around to speak to Olivia, she slipped into the adjoining bathroom. He muttered a groan, clenching his hands into fists. The frustration that had built over the whole day wore on him. At first it was just mentally, but now he could feel it in his bones and muscles.

He couldn't remember the last time he felt this on edge

over something. It should be simple to tell a woman that he was interested in her.

"Should" being the operative word there.

So why hadn't he just said it?

He needed to get his head on straight. Time was running out. If he could only find the proper words—

The bathroom door swung open and he froze.

A gasp escaped her lips and she stared at him expectantly. "I'm sorry, did you—"

He shook his head. "I need to talk to you about something."

Olivia's brow furrowed. "Okay . . ."

"I can't explain it, but I find myself strangely drawn to you."

Her eyes narrowed as she folded her arms and leaned in the doorway. "*Strangely*?"

Isaac grimaced. "I didn't mean it that way. What I'm trying to say is that there's something . . ." He shook his head as he continued to stumble over his words. Raking his hand through his hair he let out a strangled sigh. "I *like* you, Olivia."

The corners of her mouth twitched. "You *like* me."

Heat raced up the back of his neck, flooding his ears and face. "I know. There's no rhyme or reason to it. You're not my type at all. You're messy and loud. You can be a little blunt—" He glanced up at her and snapped his mouth shut. One of Olivia's brows had lifted and the faint smile was gone.

Great. He'd officially messed everything up.

For the hundredth time, he couldn't figure out what was wrong with him. Isaac laced his fingers behind his neck and groaned as he spun around to walk away. "Never mind. Forget I said anything."

"Wait a minute. You can't just say that kind of stuff to me then expect me to forget it." Olivia's voice followed him.

He stopped suddenly and faced her, causing a collision. Olivia yelped and his hands shot out to steady both of them. She blinked, staring up at him as if momentarily dazed. His grasp on her was firm enough that he couldn't tell if she attempted to pull away or not.

Olivia exhaled and her lips parted, drawing his attention to them. His blood roared in his ears, dampening all other senses. It started out as a small flicker, a hint of desire that quickly morphed into something stronger. Throat dry, he rasped, "You don't know how much I want to kiss you right now."

Color flooded her cheeks and her breath hitched.

Then again, he might have imagined that last reaction.

His voice cracked. "I didn't expect any of this to happen. But there it is. If you don't feel the same just tell—"

Olivia framed his face with both of her hands. There was a split second—a mere moment—between the time when she grabbed him and what happened next where everything slowed down. His heart stopped its incessant hammering. His stomach no longer twisted painfully. All the tension left his muscles.

And then she kissed him.

Chapter Twenty

Olivia's lashes fluttered closed as she leaned into their kiss. If it wasn't for his hold on her, she wouldn't be standing. There was no feeling left in her legs as all the blood had rushed to her head. She was strong and weak all at once. A warrior, but helpless as she offered herself to him.

Their kiss started out soft, meek, and exploratory, but swiftly increased in intensity. His lips explored hers then danced along her jawline toward her ear.

Olivia tightened her arms around him, burying her face in his neck. Their short breaths mingled, filling the air and bringing her swiftly back to reality.

The silence that grew between them wasn't as awkward as she would have expected, though she didn't dare pull away from him.

There was a battle brewing in her head over what had just happened and she needed to sort it out first and foremost.

On the one hand the logical side of her demanded an explanation. What had she done? How had she let herself fall into his arms like that? This could very well be one of the biggest mistakes of her life. There was nowhere to run to. No safe haven.

They shared a room for heaven's sake! She was halfway across the country from her home.

The argument of her heart started small but grew with ferocity. Wasn't this something that she wanted? Hadn't she been battling with similar feelings?

She'd thought Isaac to be this stuck-up guy who was only interested in things that suited his own needs. With each passing day, she'd found that not to be the case. Isaac was a decent guy. He was thoughtful and romantic.

And dang, could he kiss.

The beating of her heart agreed with resounding thunder.

Isaac was the first to step back. He shifted his grasp to her upper arms as if he knew he still needed to steady her. His gaze bore into her, searching for something she wasn't certain she was ready to give him. There were a thousand questions those eyes seemed to be asking her.

What was she supposed to say? How could she answer something she wasn't sure of herself?

Olivia let out a nervous laugh and edged out of his grasp. An apology was on the tip of her tongue but she held it back. Truth be told, she wasn't sorry.

Not even a little bit.

As if to agree to that sentiment, her face flushed hotter than the steam from a freshly brewed cup of coffee. She peeked at him then scooted toward the bed and sat, not sure if her legs would be able to hold her up much longer.

"Olivia?" he whispered, drawing her attention. His eyes sparkled and he had a crooked little grin on his face. "I don't want to assume—"

She threw her hands into the air and expelled a harsh

breath. "What do you want me to say?" Her stomach churned, bubbling and boiling over. "I like you too, okay? There. I said it." She couldn't bring herself to look at him then. She knew he'd just make fun of her.

Even still, she couldn't hold back her own small smile.

Olivia stood, using the bed to support her as she walked around it. She avoided looking at him as she pulled back the covers. "How about we finish off this week and explore what that means when we get back." This time she shot a look in his direction, hating the way he just stood in that same spot like this conversation was the most important thing in the universe. "There's a lot at stake and we don't need to complicate things. Yeah?"

He jumped into action, moving toward her, shaking his head.

She stifled a groan and held up her hand. "For once in your life, why can't you just let this be easy?"

Isaac stopped a few feet from the side of the bed. It was so sudden that her eyes cut to meet his, expecting to find anger or hurt in his gaze. But she saw none of that. He wore a mask of unreadability.

Nodding, he shifted his weight and glanced toward the bathroom. "You're right. We can figure this out later." Without another word, he reached over and grabbed a few things from his luggage and headed toward the bathroom.

Praying she hadn't just ruined the closeness they'd created, she fell back on her pillows and stared at the ceiling. There she went putting up walls again. This was her M.O. It was something she needed to work on, especially if she wanted to find someone who made her as happy as Bart made Izzie.

The shower kicked on and she rolled over onto her side,

her back facing the bathroom door. Tomorrow would be a new day—a fresh start.

A smile tugged at her lips and she touched them with her fingertips. They tingled with the memory of his touch, sending fresh waves of chills through her body. Maybe it wouldn't be so bad falling for a guy like Isaac.

Maybe this time she'd finally found someone who would stick around.

———

Olivia held her mug to her lips, staring at Isaac over the rim. Steam wafted from the coffee she held and the scent of her vanilla-peppermint creamer just made the whole morning even better.

This was probably the fifth time she'd caught him staring and each time she did, her stomach did that loop-de-loop thing she used to hate. She dragged her focus away from him and turned it to Lucille who was filling in the group on the activities planned for the rest of the week. They'd go ice skating this afternoon and tomorrow they would be preparing for the party the following day.

That meant one thing. She was going to have more one-on-one time with Isaac.

"How's your leg feeling, dear?"

Olivia jumped and focused on Lucille once more. "Pardon?"

"Your knee. Is it healing enough for this afternoon's festivities?"

"I believe so. It's still a little tender, but as long as I don't overdo it, I should be fine."

"Wonderful."

She felt his gaze on her again and bit back her laugh as their eyes met. "You're being ridiculous," she mouthed.

He shook his head.

Olivia rolled her eyes. This side of him wasn't something she ever would have expected, but she found she enjoyed it far too much to force him to return to the "normal" she was used to.

The moment breakfast was over and they were out of the kitchen, Isaac scooped her into his arms.

She let out a yelp and draped her arms around his neck. "Where are you taking me?"

"I want to show you something."

Olivia gave him a funny look. "What on earth is so important you're whisking me away like some damsel in distress? Honestly, Isaac. I'm fine to walk."

He shook his head. "And give up an opportunity to be this close to you? His brows wagged suggestively then he nuzzled her neck and murmured, "Never."

"Who are you?" She laughed as she pushed her fingers through his hair. "Because the stuffed shirt businessman I met not so long ago didn't have this kind of potential."

He let out an exaggerated gasp. "How dare you, madam. I'll have you know I have loads of potential."

"Oh yeah?"

He plopped her down on her feet and hooked his finger beneath her chin. His voice grew husky and serious. "*Loads*," he repeated. "Just you wait. One day I'll make you fall so deeply in love with me, you'll have no choice but stay with me forever."

Her throat seemed to close up and her head pounded sharply. She winced, but before she could figure out what was going on, he tugged on her hand and pulled her through an open door.

If her jaw wasn't attached, it would have fallen to the floor.

This room wasn't one they'd taken a tour of, though she couldn't imagine why. It was right in the middle of the house and it would have been silly not to utilize it during the party. The Fredericksons had created a replica of the city with those tiny little Christmas village houses. Tables and other surfaces were completely covered by quaint cottages, adorable storefronts, a large chapel, and even some iconic New York City pieces. Miniature figurines were strolling the streets, window-shopping, and ice skating.

Except for the New York-specific pieces, it looked just like that town she'd visited as a child, and her eyes soaked up every last bit of it. "This is—amazing—" She spun around only long enough to meet his eyes for a second. "How did you find out about this?" Olivia didn't wait for him to answer. She wandered along the aisles that had been set up, crouching to peer at the delicate craftsmanship of the structures. It was exquisite.

"I saw the staff putting it together yesterday. I think they're going to have it displayed for the party."

She shot a look in his direction and nodded. "I think you're right. It's just . . . wow."

A grin stretched across his face. "I thought you'd like it."

Olivia's heart flipped and her stomach followed suit. Isaac just continued to surprise her at every turn. He was thoughtful. He listened. He was the most eligible bachelor back home.

And he wanted *her*.

The warmth returned to her stomach, making her shiver. "This is really neat, Isaac." Her fingers trailed along the roof of the cathedral and then traced the edge of the mirror that had been turned into an ice-skating rink. Just looking at this brought back her happiest memories from when she was a child.

He followed her along the aisles, his closeness making her body go haywire. She let her gaze land on him every so often, always finding him watching her.

"You know, one day I'd like to get a few of these pieces. I don't think I ever considered it before but seeing all of this makes me want to look into it."

Isaac chuckled. "I don't know if that's a very good idea. I think you should probably get a bigger place first. Or maybe clean it up a little."

She gasped and whacked him with her fingertips. "How rude."

He laughed again, darting away from her so she couldn't reach him.

Olivia paused at a small cottage that was situated away from the rest of the town. A memory from her childhood accosted her. The caroling she'd done with her family. A house on the outskirts of town. The pretty young couple who'd stood in the doorway and offered them a plate of cookies. The woman was pregnant and Olivia had been enthralled with her.

That memory had been buried so deep, but now that it had floated to the surface, all she could do was think about was how much she'd wanted a family like that all her own. A small home away from the city, and a good man.

Years later, she'd grown so jaded. What had happened to the woman who wanted that kind of life? She'd realized people weren't predictable and eventually they all left. Olivia found herself looking at him again.

Maybe she'd been wrong this whole time.

Maybe Isaac was different.

Chapter Twenty-One

The Christmas village had gone well, but Isaac had come up with another surprise to make this trip memorable for Olivia. The thing she most wanted to do while she was here was to go caroling in the snow. At the time that she'd insisted they do it, he hadn't planned on fulfilling that wish. He'd had a one-track mind, and catering to that woman wasn't on his list.

Things had changed.

Based on the schedule they had planned, he might be able to take her the night before the party. Mr. Frederickson hadn't been available much today for Isaac to speak to, but Isaac intended on asking the man about it.

If there was one person who would be up for making the romantic happen, it was Mr. Frederickson.

That evening, as they put on their skates at the rink, he hovered near Olivia, making sure she wasn't overdoing it. His eyes remained trained on her feet as she laced up the skates tight enough to make him flinch.

Her eyes darted up to meet his and she laughed. "I'm fine! I *promise*. My knee barely hurts anymore. I'm more than capable of skating with you. I'm not going to ruin the night just because of some silly mistake I made." Her face flushed and he was certain her thoughts had returned to the night in question.

Isaac held out his hand to her and helped her to her feet. They got onto the ice and glided hand in hand, taking it slowly. Overhead the sky was clear and stars glimmered. This could be his future. What was once something he thought he'd never want was suddenly within his reach.

Olivia leaned into him, their pace slowing. She let out a sigh. "Don't you think this is crazy?"

He chuckled. "What? Ice-skating on a swollen ankle?"

She nudged him. "*No.* How this all started. This. You and me. Old Olivia would be appalled at what is happening." She snickered. "If someone had told me a week ago that I'd be holding your hand, contemplating our future, I would have told them they were nuts."

His arm slipped around her waist keeping her secured against him. "I think things happen for a reason, and sometimes we never get to know the why. We just need to accept them."

Olivia craned her head around and stared at him with a narrowed gaze. "I thought you said there was no such thing as luck."

"I didn't say anything about things happening because of luck. I said they happen sometimes without any rhyme or reason."

She rolled her eyes. "That's basically the same thing."

He tilted his head. "I think of it as serendipity."

"Agree to disagree." Olivia laughed again. She was quiet for a little while as they continued their way on the ice. Her voice turned somber. "I didn't know your father left your mom. She never said anything."

He stiffened. Of course he knew she'd been listening when he'd given that information to the Tillies. But having her bring it up was still awkward. He cleared his throat and glanced down at her. "Yeah. I didn't expect she would have said anything. It happened a long time ago."

She nodded. "Sure. That makes sense." More silence. What did she think of him now? Would she judge him for his inability to cope with his parents' breakup? Olivia's eyes met his and she offered him a smile that didn't reach her eyes. "I guess we make quite a pair, huh?"

"Why do you say that?"

"We're both a little damaged."

He tugged her to a stop and took both of her hands within his. "You're not damaged."

She tilted her head and let out a strangled laugh. "You don't have to say that. I know I am. In fact, I'd challenge you to find even one person who doesn't have some kind of baggage. We've figured out how to live through it, though. So I guess that means we're pretty strong, too."

Isaac studied her. While she appeared to be experiencing some sadness, it wasn't so much that he thought she needed soothing. There were no words he could say to make her feel better, because, for the most part, he agreed with her.

He pulled her hard against his chest and rested his chin on her head, ignoring the skaters that passed by them. Yes, they both had baggage. But she was not damaged goods. He could tell her that until he was blue in the face, but she would never accept it.

So he'd just have to prove it to her.

Her arms slipped around him and she held onto him. The white puffs from their breathing swirled around them, protecting them from the world surrounding them. Right now, they were in a bubble created by the newness of their relationship. The real trial would come when they returned home.

Even as she held tightly to him, he couldn't help but feel that something was off. It was as if she'd gotten something in her mind and she'd latched onto it. Isaac had a sixth sense about these things. It was what made him so good at his business.

But his relationship with Olivia was different than any other in his life. It was possible that he was allowing himself to overreact. He needed to squash those concerns before they became a bigger issue and pushed her away.

Olivia pulled back and he pressed a kiss to her forehead before she slipped her hand into his and they continued skating. Her cheeks colored and she let out a laugh. "What are we going to do when we get back?"

He stiffened. "What do you mean?" Isaac's hand tightened around hers. "I'm going to take you to a nice dinner and we're going to continue seeing each other."

She laughed again, shaking her head. "No. What are we going to do about Izzie and Bart?"

Tilting his head, he squinted at her. "You . . . want to do something with them?"

"What are we going to *tell* them? You know Izzie isn't going to let me live this down. I'm pretty sure Bart will be right there with her."

His smile spread. "I think they'd be happy for us."

"Happy? It's gonna be more like an 'I told you so.'"

Isaac shook his head. Her worries were nothing if not amusing. "You don't like it when other people prove you wrong, do you?"

She dropped his hand and distanced herself from him,

her eyes dancing with delight. "Don't you know? I'm always right."

"Is that so?"

Olivia nodded. "One way or the other." She shrugged, the glee still written on her face. "Guess I'm just lucky."

He launched toward her, grasping her hands and pulling her close again. "There's no such thing as luck."

"Then maybe I'm just super smart." Her voice lowered and their eyes locked. The humor in the air between them thickened into something different—something more palpable.

Her eyes shone with it, drawing him in. Her full lips inviting him to taste her. Even with the breeze tugging at her hair, she appeared angelic. Pure and straight from heaven.

The corners of his lips quirked upward. "You're *so* beautiful." He grasped her chin with his finger and thumb then leaned closer to her.

"Come on, lovebirds. We're about ready to head back."

He turned toward the voice, finding Mrs. Tillie with her hands on her hips and a wide smile on her face. Isaac mumbled a groan which made Olivia chuckle.

She scooted back and tugged on his hand. "Come on. It's getting late and I'm getting tired."

"But I wanted a kiss," he muttered.

Olivia tossed her head back and laughed. Then she leaned forward and pecked him on the cheek.

He pouted. "That's not what I meant and you know it."

Olivia yawned as the car came to a stop in front of the Fredericksons' property. She'd rested her head on his shoulder for the whole ride and every so often Mr. Frederickson would meet Isaac's eyes and offer him a smile.

Just before they exited the vehicle, Mr. Frederickson leaned forward. "When you have a moment, I'd like to see you in my office."

Isaac nodded. "Of course, sir."

He left Olivia prepping to take a hot bath and skipped down the stairs.

Eventually he found the right door and knocked.

"Come in."

Isaac pushed open the door and poked his head inside.

"Ah, Isaac, take a seat." Mr. Frederickson gestured toward a small couch set up in front of a coffee table on the side of the room. Every wall was lined with bookshelves that reached the ceiling except where there was a large window with bay seating.

The moon shone through the opening, and the only other light in the room was from the few lamps that Mr. Frederickson had turned on. He rose from his desk and moved toward the couch, opting to sit in a chair that faced it.

Isaac sat stiffly in his seat. It took everything in his power not to fidget while sitting in front of this man who could dictate the future of Maple Gardens. He needed to show an air of confidence if he wanted to convince the man an investment was a wise decision.

Mr. Frederickson's features broke into a wide smile. "I'm sorry I haven't had more time to visit with you on this investment opportunity of yours."

"Oh, it's really not a big deal," Isaac assured him. "You have all the information at your fingertips. I'm just here if you have any questions."

Mr. Frederickson held up a folder. "That I do. I've had

my people look over it and we can't find anything that would persuade us to walk away from such an offer."

Isaac's heart thundered. It couldn't be this easy, could it?

Olivia's voice flooded his thoughts. Her disappointment in his lying dragged down the excitement that had been building from the second he entered the office. He pushed aside those disparaging thoughts. It wasn't really a lie—not anymore.

He settled back on the cushion, taking a deep breath to settle his nerves. "That's great."

"I wanted to tell you how impressed I've been with you and Miss Todd. Coming to stay with almost complete strangers and their other guests."

"Of course. Anything to put your mind at ease. You're the exact kind of investor who could help make Maple Gardens a household name."

This was actually happening.

Isaac almost couldn't believe it.

But there was something else that surprised him more.

The only person he wanted to tell was waiting upstairs.

He couldn't wait to head back to his room and tell Olivia all about it.

Mr. Frederickson placed the file on the table between them and smiled broadly. "I wanted to let you know that I'm having my lawyers put together an offer for you to look over while you're here. Of course you won't have to accept it right away. I would expect you'd like to have your own lawyers go over it. But for now"—he leaned forward and extended his hand—"let's shake on our future partnership."

Isaac accepted his hand and shook it firmly. "Thank

you, Mr. Frederickson. I'm looking forward to working with you."

He took the stairs two at a time and practically jogged down the hall toward their room. He swung the door wide then shut. Olivia stood at the window, staring out into the night. She turned when the door clicked and his happiness faltered. There was a crease between her brows like she'd been thinking about something upsetting.

Isaac crossed the floor more slowly than he'd planned. He didn't like the way she was looking at him. Immediately his thoughts shifted to everything he'd gained over the last week and it felt like that could all be wiped away.

"What's wrong?"

She gave her head a sharp shake. "Nothing. It's . . . nothing."

"No. There's something wrong. I can tell."

Olivia sighed. "We're going home in a few days."

"Yes . . ." he drawled, "and that bothers you because . . ."

She lifted a shoulder. "I guess I'm scared."

"You're scared." This was not where he'd thought she would go with this conversation.

A harsh breath escaped her lips and she moved her head back to look out the window. "What if we get home and everything changes? We're here in this beautiful place with forced proximity." She whirled around to face him. "Can you honestly say that we would have found this—whatever it is—"

"Love."

Her eyes darted to meet his, then pulled away. "Do you think we would have found love if we weren't in this exact situation?"

Isaac moved closer to her, his whole body on edge. It might have been the stark contrast of that high he'd come down from after his meeting with Mr. Frederickson. Or the more likely cause of his anxiety—the utter wonder of being in a relationship at all. It was compounded by the fact that he found he truly cared for Olivia. He wanted her in his life so much he'd even toyed with the fantasy of starting a family with her.

The back of his throat burned and he swallowed hard to get some semblance of relief. "I don't care how we came to be in love. I just care that it happened. People meet under the strangest circumstances. This is just one of those moments." He reached for her hand and trailed his thumb over the back of it. Her skin was soft and pale. Sometimes he saw her as this delicate flower but then she'd do something out of the norm and completely throw him off. And he was still just getting to know the inner workings of what made her the woman he was falling for.

When he lifted his gaze to meet hers, the furrow of her brow was gone, replaced by something more serene. "You're probably right."

"What did Mr. Frederickson want?"

A slow smile spread across his face. "Wait 'til you hear this."

Chapter Twenty-Two

Everything was working out exactly as it was supposed to. So why did Olivia have this sick feeling in her gut? Why couldn't she get these obsessive thoughts out of her head? This always happened. Something good came along and she always found a way to ruin it. So as Isaac continued with his excited chatter, she focused on pushing down the thoughts of worry.

The following day, she could still sense that something had shifted between them, but with all the running around that was going on to prepare for the party, she didn't have much of a chance to fix it.

There was one thing weighing on her, however. Throughout the whole deep and meaningful she'd had with Isaac the other night, not once did he mention whether he'd tell Mr. Frederickson the truth. The notion was ridiculous. How could she expect him to say something when he'd finally gotten what he wanted?

And why does this matter so much?

Not only that, but they *were* technically in some kind of relationship now.

Would it be so bad to keep this little secret from his investor?

But little secrets become big ones. What if thinks he can keep secrets from me?

This wasn't some small thing. From what she understood, this investment was worth millions. The expansion of Maple Gardens was going to be huge. And as she sat across the table from Isaac, studying him while he chatted with Mr. Tillie about this exact issue, she couldn't help but feel that something needed to be said.

It wasn't her place. She wasn't the one lying to seal a multi-million-dollar deal.

But she was an accomplice.

Now that this investment was happening, she felt sick. She'd helped trick their hosts.

What will he want me to do next time he needs to lie?

"Aren't you hungry, dear? It's been a long day with all of the preparations. I would imagine you were starving." Lucille nodded toward her plate.

All eyes were on her now, noting how she'd moved her food around her plate but hadn't actually eaten anything. Olivia smiled at her host and put her fork down. "You know, I'm exhausted. I think I'll head to bed early."

Isaac jumped from his seat the second she stood. "Are you sure, I had something—"

She nodded. "Don't worry about me. I'm fine. Just a little tired. I'll be right as rain for the party tomorrow."

Isaac hesitated. Those seated at the table glanced between him and Olivia. She didn't dare meet his gaze for long. If he sensed how dark her feelings had become, there was no telling what kind of argument they might have.

She needed to figure a few things out before she made any lasting decisions. Lying had always been a big thing to her. She despised it. People were never who they said they were. In the end none of them could be counted on. It was a slippery slope and she knew it.

The Fredericksons think they can count on Isaac. Count on me.

Olivia brushed a strand of hair from her face and left the room. She needed to get out of there before anything bad happened. Her heart fluttered and the dismal thoughts continued to snowball. It had to stop.

She was okay.

They were okay.

Letting this one instance come between them would be utterly ridiculous.

Olivia reached her room and immediately locked herself in the bathroom in case Isaac followed her. Fortunately, after waiting for about ten minutes, she found herself alone. Either he didn't notice how much she was struggling with her doubts, or he didn't care enough to push her to confront them.

It almost felt like her childhood all over again.

How many times did she have to work through her disappointments with her foster family? How many times was she lied to?

Olivia dug her hands into her hair and took a deep breath. This was different. Isaac was different. If she asked him to come clean with Mr. Frederickson, he probably would.

She lifted her head, her thoughts finally clearing. She was making such a big deal about this when she hadn't even bothered to ask him to confess. She didn't know much, but she felt she knew enough about him to assume he'd do the right thing.

Her heart felt lighter. The headache lessened. Olivia left

the bathroom and got dressed for bed. She picked up her fuzzy red slippers and grinned. She could see herself telling the story of how she came all the way to New York in December with nothing to wear on her feet except these slippers, and Isaac had forced her to get proper footwear.

With the lights turned out, she climbed into bed and curled up on her side. Isaac didn't return to their room until much later, but she hadn't fallen asleep yet. He moved through the darkness with his phone as a flashlight. At one point he tripped over a pair of shoes and let out a quiet curse.

She grinned, the blankets tugged up to her chin. She'd tell him tomorrow what she needed and everything would be set right.

Olivia dragged her hands down her dress and turned so she could get the full effect in the mirror. She still couldn't believe that Isaac had insisted on buying this. It was officially the most expensive thing she owned and she absolutely loved it.

But that was how Isaac was. He was generous and kind-hearted. And as soon as she talked with him about clearing this whole thing up with Mr. Frederickson, everything would be perfect. She hadn't been able to ask him earlier. There just didn't seem like enough time.

He'd been pulled into a meeting with Mr. Tillie and Mr. Frederickson right after lunch, so she spent her afternoon primping for the big party that was just about to start.

There was a knock at the bathroom door and she gave herself one more cursory look before she pulled it open.

Isaac's gaze swept over her appreciatively and he let out

a whistle. "Wow." He stepped forward and took her hand, spinning her in a circle. "I knew the dress was going to look good, but I never imagined it would be this amazing. You look . . . just *wow*."

She blushed as he tugged her toward him and slipped his arms around her waist. Her fingers splayed on his chest and her heart thundered. Now was the perfect time to bring up her concerns. They'd be leaving soon and he wouldn't want to discuss this sort of thing over the phone with Mr. Frederickson.

"Isaac?" she murmured as she forced herself to meet his eye line. "I wanted to ask you something."

His brows furrowed but he didn't seem to shy away from her. He nodded, indicating that she should go ahead.

She opened her mouth but the words wouldn't come. Someone knocked on the door and as one they turned their attention in that direction.

Isaac held up a finger, releasing her as he headed for the door. There were quiet voices and then he shut the door. "Looks like we're being summoned."

"But—"

He crossed the room and grasped her hand. Bringing it to his lips, he smiled. "Can you tell me later tonight? We need to get out there so Mr. Frederickson can introduce me."

"Introduce you?"

Isaac nodded. "Most of the guests are people he works with. He wants to announce the plans for Maple Gardens."

Olivia's stomach bottomed out as he tugged her toward the door. Her feet shuffled along the floor as they headed out of the room and into the hallway. All her nerve disappeared just like that and the sick feeling in her gut returned. She'd find another way to tell him. He'd understand. Even as she tried to convince herself of this, she wasn't so sure anymore.

———————

"You want me to *what?*"

Olivia was wrong. He didn't understand. From their spot behind the buffet, she glanced around the party to see if they'd drawn anyone's attention.

"I can't do that and you know why." Isaac gently took her upper arm and guided her toward the Christmas tree that graced the corner of the room. His voice was almost low enough to be a growl. "This is what we came for, Olivia. What we both came for."

"And he's not going to change his mind now that he knows you."

Uncertainty flickered in Isaac's eyes but then he shook his head. "It's too risky."

Olivia pulled her arm from his grasp and folded it with the other across her chest. "You know my feelings on this subject. From the beginning I—"

"You what? We have a business arrangement and I need you to keep your end of it."

"*Exactly*. You *hired* me," she hissed. "You can't expect me to be okay with it after things have changed."

"The point is that they have changed. We are in a relationship. It's not really a lie anymore."

She gasped. "You didn't just say that."

"I don't understand what you mean."

Heat seared her face and she placed her hand on her forehead. "All of this was a lie to begin with. That's the point. You need to let him know that—"

He groaned. "I'm not going to tell him anything. It

won't help anyone. His reasoning for not wanting to invest was unreasonable and judgmental. He wanted me to be in a committed relationship. Well, now I am. So how can it matter if I wasn't dating you officially when we arrived?" He pinched the bridge of his nose. "Honestly, you're being ridiculous."

Her mouth dropped open but she recovered quickly. Eyes narrowing, she pressed her lips into a thin line. This was what she'd been afraid of. Excuses and inability to take ownership for something. Lies. If he was willing to commit this kind of deceit with his business decisions, what other levels of lies would he hide from her?

Olivia spun around and charged away from him. Her face was hot and her hands were shaking. She didn't know if she'd be able to make it up the stairs without tripping. Either way, she wasn't going to stay here a second longer.

"Olivia!" His voice was close.

She hadn't heard his approach over the volume of the music playing. She jumped but didn't give him her focus.

"What are you doing?" He spoke through gritted teeth, a sign he was only holding back because they had witnesses. "People are watching."

She stopped and faced him, fury sparking in every crevice of her body. "Let them watch."

His head reared back. "You can't be serious. You're going to make a scene—to what—make a point? There is no point to be made."

"Oh yes there is. We're not dating. We never were. Did we have some good moments? Sure. But that was quickly overtaken by your pride and inflexibility." She shook her head. "You know? You almost had me fooled. You *almost* had me believing that you were different and I was wrong to judge you. But I was right all along. You're a spoiled rich man who only cares about himself and his business. You don't care about anyone else and I was a fool for thinking otherwise." She brushed past him then stopped short. Standing before her was Lucille, and one of her staff who held a large punchbowl.

Lucille stared at her then shifted her attention to Isaac. She didn't say a word and they all remained frozen until Olivia couldn't take the scrutiny any longer. "I'm so sorry, Lucille. I'm unable to stay for the duration of the party. I'll be leaving tonight." She brushed past the stunned woman, only vaguely hearing Isaac's low voice as he said something to her.

She kicked off her shoes and bent down to grasp them with her fingers. The cold tile soothed her feet and seemed to cool her body temperature slightly. Olivia ran toward the stairs. Her hair fell from its pins but she didn't care. No one would have to see her this way. She'd slip out the side, call a cab, and head back to Georgia where the world made sense.

There was no time to change. She had to get out of there before she did something she would truly regret. There was no way she'd get paid after the stunt she pulled so her only option was to get out ahead of this.

The second she entered the room, she locked the door. Then she made quick work of throwing what she could easily get her hands on into the suitcase she'd brought. At this point it didn't matter if she forgot anything. She just wanted to get out of there.

She was just leaning on her suitcase to close it and zip it shut when a pounding at the door interrupted her. Olivia jumped, freezing in her place.

"*Olivia*," Isaac called, "come on, let's talk this through."

Shaking her head, she worked at loosening the stubborn zipper that had gotten stuck on part of the suitcase.

"What are you doing? I didn't mean for this to upset you." His voice softened but she could still hear it through the wood. There, along with the frustration, was a desperation, and it tore at her heart to hear it.

Olivia shut her eyes and took a deep breath. She could do this. All she had to do was get past him and out to a cab. She could call a taxi now so she wouldn't have to be seen waiting on the front steps of this place. Then she could go before her heart broke into a million pieces.

Chapter Twenty-Three

Isaac paced outside the door to the room he shared with Olivia. He'd raked his hand through his hair so many times he was sure he looked an utter mess. Mr. Frederickson was bound to know by now what had transpired between the two of them. Lucille would have told him.

But that didn't matter anymore. Olivia was slipping through his fingers.

He would lose her.

Just like he'd lost his father.

He stilled, staring at the door. Maybe it was better if she left before they said anything that would hurt each other more. There was no way to meet in the middle on this subject.

His pacing resumed. Voices and music still drifted up from the main level. It sure didn't seem like their little outburst had ruined the ambiance of the party. At least there was that. Maybe he still had a shot at smoothing everything out. Olivia was a smart woman, she could be reasoned with. She just had to let him talk to her. He'd make her see how much this deal meant to Maple Gardens.

And how much you mean to me.

Isaac stopped and moved to the door, resting his forehead against it. "Olivia. Let's talk about this. We can still go out there and fix this. We can just tell them it was a joke."

Joke? Did I just say that?

The door swung open and he had to catch himself on the doorjamb. Her face was flushed red and her eyes sparked fire. "Fix this? What do you mean, *fix* this? You can't honestly be suggesting we go back in there and tell them we were joking around when all along it was our relationship which is the joke!"

"Our relationship? No—"

She held up her hand. "I can't believe you. No, wait. I *can* believe it. Because this is exactly what someone like you would do. You will blame anyone but yourself. You know what? No. I'm not going anywhere with you." The phone in her hand buzzed and she lifted it up. "In fact, my taxi is here. I'm catching a plane and I hope I never see you again." Olivia disappeared into their room then burst out the door dragging her suitcase behind her.

"Olivia, wait." He hurried after her, dodging around the obstacle she somehow managed to use as a shield. "You can't just leave." He reached for her hand.

"The heck I can't." Olivia tore her hand from his grasp and shoved the handle into the suitcase. She held onto it tightly and struggled down the stairs. When he offered to take it from her, she glowered at him. "Don't."

Isaac stepped back, letting her take the lead. He followed her, two steps behind until they got to the main level. She darted toward the front door, bypassing the room where everyone was still mingling. He hurried after her and they both ended up out in the cold standing side by side.

Her ride wasn't there. It must have been a false alarm.

Olivia shivered, one arm wrapping around her body. In her haste to leave, she had neglected to grab her coat. Or maybe she'd left it behind on purpose.

"Olivia?" he whispered, "do you think we could talk about this now?"

She shook her head.

"Okay, do you think I could talk about it and you could just . . . listen?"

Olivia eyed him but didn't refuse.

He took a deep breath but it did nothing to settle his mind or his heart. His thoughts whirled in every direction, not able to compartmentalize like he needed it to. His ability to prioritize what was important was lost. His heart was torn between trying to save the relationship they'd only just discovered and trying to decide what to do about Mr. Frederickson.

Shifting his weight from one foot to the other, he glanced at her. Her teeth started chattering and snow flurries fluttered around them. Isaac shrugged out of his suit jacket and draped it around her. All at once he knew what needed to happen. He couldn't ask her to stay. Not after what had just occurred. They weren't right for each other.

Too many differences. Too much baggage.

Too stubborn to give in.

"Maybe you're making a good point."

She stiffened and finally met his gaze fully.

He didn't mean it in the way she wanted him to. He could see the hope in her eyes and it nearly broke his heart. "This isn't going to work and it would probably be best if we just didn't see each other anymore." His throat closed up and he tore his gaze away. A set of headlights flashed at them from down the street.

"Isaac—"

He shook his head. The fact of the matter was that he'd always prioritized his work, and for good reason. He could always count on it working out the way he needed it to. His business wasn't fickle—not in the way people were. It wouldn't lose its temper and it didn't get its feelings hurt. He couldn't give her what she needed and he'd never really wanted a relationship.

Until her, his heart reminded him.

Isaac shoved that thought down into the depths of his soul, surrounding it with a brick wall and locking it in a box, never to be opened again.

Olivia faced him just as the taxi arrived. Her face was pinched with pain and uncertainty. It was almost like he'd called her bluff. Only, he knew that wasn't possible. Olivia had good instincts. She knew when something wasn't good for her.

The taxi stopped and he moved toward it, pulling the door open for her.

"Isaac—"

"I'm not good for you." His words echoed his dismal thoughts. "I never was and I never will be. You need more in your life than what I can offer. And I need something from you that you aren't able to give."

"You're not making any sense."

He gestured toward the house. "That business deal is the only reason I came here. This thing we had . . . it was fun. But it's not conducive to the life I lead. You can understand that."

Isaac couldn't tell if the color in her cheeks was from the cold or her unhappiness. There was only one thing he knew for certain. It was in her eyes. The way she looked at him. She hated him in this moment. More than she'd hated him when they'd had their argument. More than she hated him when he stood outside the bedroom door.

In this moment, he was the scum of the earth.

He reached for the luggage and moved around to the open trunk that the driver had unlatched. Isaac shut the suitcase inside and let his hand linger on the cold vehicle. He'd made hard decisions before. And this was no different. He couldn't force her to be with him when she deserved better.

Olivia was still standing out in the freezing air, her eyes cold as the ice that surrounded them. He gestured toward the taxi. "I hope you have a safe flight." He turned and headed inside without looking back at her. The door shut and the tires spun on the ice. When he shot a look over his shoulder, she was gone.

Isaac couldn't bring himself to go back to the party. He also couldn't exactly escape like Olivia had just done. His hosts didn't deserve that. He had to apologize and plead his case. He'd lost so much already, he couldn't lose the deal he'd just made.

Now was not the time to do that, however. He needed to let the guests enjoy their party and he'd have a sit-down with the Fredericksons in the morning.

He made it back to his room and shut the door. The chill from outside hadn't worn off, but that was fine. He didn't mind feeling numb. It was probably for the best anyway. He needed to get back into the right mindset so he would be sharp tomorrow.

The room felt colder without Olivia or her things here,

but there were still signs of her everywhere. The bed wasn't made, the pillows were in a haphazard mess on the floor.

The place where she'd kept her open suitcase was bare. Travel-size shampoo bottles were still scattered on the bathroom counter.

Since when had he become so nostalgic? This was but a moment in his life. There were so many others he'd had that were more important. And yet, his heart ached with each beat that stuttered in his chest.

He tugged at his tie, loosening it as he moved across the room toward the pillow. Isaac scooped it up and something red caught his eye. Once more, he stooped down as he picked up one of her annoying, red, fuzzy slippers. He snorted as he turned it over in his hands. This was the symbol of everything he found infuriating about her—and yet he couldn't deny that he'd just lost something special.

Isaac yanked his tie from his neck and tossed it along with the slipper onto the bed. As if on autopilot, he undressed and changed into jeans. He'd need to schedule a return flight to Georgia as soon as he could and get back to work. He might as well get his things packed and ready.

It would have been nice to wait until morning to be confronted by Mr. Frederickson, but luck wasn't on his side tonight. About nine o'clock, there was a knock on his door. He peered at the door as if he had x-ray vision but there was no telling who was on the other side. His best guess was that the Fredericksons would ask him to take his leave after embarrassing them at their party.

Another knock.

He groaned and got to his feet. It was only a matter of time. He'd realized that the second he left the party and chased after Olivia. He'd messed everything up and the ironic thing was that he hadn't seen this coming. He was losing his touch.

Isaac opened the door and froze.

Mr. Frederickson hadn't been up to his room since he'd arrived. He hadn't given a tour up this way, nor had he come to get him for any activity. He'd gotten to the point where he'd assumed the man didn't like going to the second story of his own home.

But there he was, still dressed in his party attire, standing there himself instead of sending the butler to come retrieve Isaac.

Isaac straightened and tried to smooth his mussed hair. "Sir, if I had known you wanted to see me, I would have come to you." Okay, he knew Frederickson would want to have a word with him, he'd just expected it to happen tomorrow. The party was still ongoing downstairs. To have the host leave his own party meant he was probably really upset.

Gesturing toward the bedroom, he let out a strained chuckle. "Would you like to come in? Or would you prefer we have this conversation in your office?"

Mr. Frederickson had his hands in his pockets and he rocked back on his heels. "I'm guessing you know why I'm here."

Isaac nodded, swallowing back the anxiety that suddenly overwhelmed him. "I have a good idea, yes."

Mr. Frederickson jerked his chin down the hall. "How about we just take a walk."

"I feel a little underdressed to be wandering the halls of your home—"

"Nonsense." He started walking, leaving Isaac to follow him without another word.

Isaac jumped into action, closing his bedroom door and jogging to catch up with his host.

Mr. Frederickson didn't speak and Isaac wondered if the man was giving him an opportunity to get ahead of this. Then again, he might just be waiting for a moment to sandbag him with the information he likely got straight from his wife. Either way, Isaac preferred to play defense. If he knew exactly what Mr. Frederickson was upset about, he might be able to give options to make the situation better.

The man placed his hands behind his back and their steps slowed. He glanced at Isaac out of the corner of his eye and chuckled. "I get the feeling that things are a little rocky between you and Miss Todd."

Isaac stiffened. While that was accurate, it wasn't what he'd expected at all. "Sir, you must be mistaken—"

"I remember the first fight I had with Lucille." The skin around his eyes wrinkled as he smiled. "And boy, it was a doozy."

Isaac didn't know how to respond. Had Lucille misunderstood the argument he'd had with Olivia? He snapped his mouth shut and waited for Mr. Frederickson to continue.

"That woman could make the earth stop spinning if she wanted to." Mr. Frederickson winked. "It's just a good thing that she doesn't use her power for evil."

"Sir?"

Mr. Frederickson stopped as they came to the end of the hall and stood beside a window. The darkness outside made it near impossible to see much of anything but the lights that had been strung on the trees and throughout the garden. "Whatever it is that has happened between you and Miss Todd, I suggest you fix it."

"You don't understand—"

He placed his hands on Isaac's shoulders and gave him a smile. "I understand more than you think I do. You forget that I've been hanging around since you arrived. This *is* my home."

"But sir—"

"Let me finish. I'm fully aware there were certain things that were said between us. Certain things that weren't completely true. I only have one question for you."

Isaac swallowed hard but it did nothing to relieve the pressure in his throat. His head was spinning from the direction this conversation had taken. This was the moment he'd been expecting and it had come far too soon. He hadn't even had time to regroup and come up with an excuse that Mr. Frederickson might accept.

"That girl—you love her, yes?"

Isaac opened his mouth, ready to spew anything that might get him out of this situation but he was so caught off guard all he could do was nod while his mouth hung open.

"Then what in the world are you doing here?"

Isaac snapped his mouth shut. He frowned as he looked away from his host. "I don't think she wants anything to do with me."

"So?"

"That sort of thing might have worked when you were young. But today, the women are built different—the men too, for that matter. We don't compromise."

"Well, that's your problem, you nincompoop."

Isaac's head whipped around and he stared at Mr. Frederickson with surprise. What was he supposed to say to that?

"That woman has feelings for you. She cares about you. I would wager she would stand by your side no matter the cost. But you have to be the kind of guy she can stand beside. Own up to your mistakes and win her back."

It wasn't that easy. There was no way he could convince Mr. Frederickson of that either. The man was insisting that all Isaac had to do was show up at the airport and tell her he loved her then everything would work out.

Well, this wasn't a fairytale and he wasn't Prince Charming.

"What if she doesn't want to take me back?"

Mr. Frederickson lifted a shoulder. "Then at least you can say you tried." He patted Isaac on the shoulder. "We've still got a deal either way. Not that this means I want you lying about your relationships. I can see my part in this and Lucille already gave me a tongue lashing for it. I expect complete honesty—even if that means that you might disappoint me. You're a good man, Spencer. I'll be seeing you back in Georgia after the holidays." He patted Isaac's shoulder once more. "Have a merry Christmas."

Isaac stared after him, dumbfounded. Either the guy was completely crazy, or he was a saint. There was no telling which it was. He leaned against the wall, letting his head fall against the plaster behind him. Olivia wouldn't be speaking to him any time soon, and after their last conversation, he wasn't so sure he could handle another like it.

He'd been a fool to think he could have it all. It was time to hang up his notions of finding someone to spend the rest of his life with. He would always be a bachelor.

Chapter Twenty-Four

Lights twinkled on the enormous tree that sat front and center in the reception area. Every wall and spare surface was decked out in evergreen garland and berries. Pine scent saturated every square inch of Maple Gardens and it only made Olivia sick to her stomach.

She sat in reception, her elbow on the counter and her cheek in her hand. Staffing was understandably low, but that was fine since most of the residents had been checked out for holiday festivities.

It was quiet, except for the sound of Christmas music playing over the speakers and the occasional resident wandering in from the cold to play bingo.

Olivia spun the chair around. She rested her head back and her thoughts drifted once again to her trip with Isaac. Every time that happened, her heart sagged and her lungs tightened.

Izzie said she'd been too harsh on him. Yes, he'd lied to his investor, but in the end it wasn't a lie.

Just because a lie became a truth didn't mean it was suddenly okay. Isaac should have made things right with the guy who was supposed to trust him. That wasn't too demanding of a request. How was she supposed to trust him when she knew he could change his story at any minute?

She spun some more, closing her eyes against the dizzying swirl of colors. It had been two weeks and she hadn't been fired. So Isaac *had* been honest about that—he wasn't going to make her lose her job. She was back to square one.

No money.

No boyfriend.

No family.

A sigh burst from her lips as she allowed her chair to come to a slow stop. A floating head buzzed past her vision once, twice, and Olivia gasped. She slammed her feet on the floor and stood up, her face bursting with heat. Her vision blurred and she had to grasp the edge of the counter with both hands until she found her equilibrium.

Millie Spencer stood at the counter smiling sweetly. She wore a bright red sweater with little snowmen on it. "Hello, dear."

"Um, Millie. What can I do for you?"

"I was just wondering if my son has arrived yet?"

The blood drained from Olivia's face, only adding to the disorientation she felt. "Isaac—Mr. Spencer?"

"He said he'd be coming in today to spend some time with me after he finishes some big deal at work."

A sour taste filled Olivia's mouth. Another *deal*. The guy was insatiable. She forced a smile and her voice went up an octave. "That's nice."

Millie remained in her place, staring expectantly at Olivia. There was no way Millie didn't know about her little getaway with Isaac based on the way her eyes seemed to stare right into Olivia's soul.

Olivia cleared her throat and shifted her weight from foot to food. "Nope. I haven't seen him. Is there anything else I can do for you?"

Millie still didn't move. "I was hoping you could answer a few questions for me."

This was not where she thought this conversation would go. Immediately her thoughts turned to Isaac. Had he mentioned her? What was Millie's opinion of the lies they'd participated in together?

Olivia swallowed hard and nodded. "Sure. What do you need?"

Millie's face broke into a bright smile. "Wonderful. Come sit with me." She didn't wait for a response, instead she headed straight for a table near the Christmas tree. Olivia shot a look around the room once, then twice, before she let out a heavy sigh and trudged over to the table. Who was she kidding? Millie knew everything and this conversation would go one of two ways. She'd be upset that Olivia had participated in the first place. Or she'd be upset at the way it had ended.

Both would end up with Olivia being put between a rock and a hard place. She genuinely liked Millie, but something told her that their little friendship was coming to an end. There was no way to get around it. The way Millie sat at that table waving Olivia over, she knew without a doubt there would be a shift occurring between the two of them. No amount of courage would help her here. She just needed to sit down and hear Millie out.

Olivia sat across from Millie and placed her hands in her lap. There was no hiding her apprehension, but to her surprise, Millie's demeanor remained bright and cheery.

"Don't look so terrified, dear. I simply would like to know what went wrong."

"I beg your pardon?"

She laughed. "You don't have to play coy. I was the one who told Isaac you would make a great candidate for his . . ." She looked side to side, leaned forward, and lowered her voice. "Predicament."

Olivia's eyes widened. Millie's confession pulled everything together. Initially she had thought Isaac had picked her because he didn't have many options, but this made more sense. "You?"

Millie grinned and nodded. Then she shook her head. "Well, not just me. Alice and Lily too. We had a hand in other matches around here, too." Her grin faded into a concerned frown. "That's why I wanted to know what went wrong. We were so certain of your match; you can imagine my surprise when Isaac didn't say a thing when he got back."

Squirming in her seat, Olivia tore her focus from the woman to her hands in her lap. "I guess it's my fault."

"Nonsense. It takes two to tango. Isaac refuses to talk to me about it—"

"Mom! What do you think you're doing?"

Olivia stiffened and time slowed down to a crawl. The hairs on the back of her neck stood on end. Just hearing his voice again set her heart racing. Every part of her was on fire from her face to her hands to her feet. His voice had come from behind and Millie was looking right above her shoulder.

She couldn't turn around. If she had to look into his eyes, see his face again, she didn't know what would happen. What was worse, she wasn't sure if she could handle seeing him angry with her, which was most likely of all.

Swallowing hard, she remained frozen in her seat. Her heart continued to pound itself into oblivion.

Then everything sped up. Millie's smile did nothing to soothe Olivia's mind. She patted the space at the table between herself and Olivia. "Come sit down, Isaac. This has to do with you, too."

Isaac didn't move. He seemed to be caught in whatever this magic was that prevented them from being able to move their bodies.

Millie's pointed look finally got things moving. Isaac let out a heavy breath and moved around Olivia. He pulled out the chair and settled into it. Olivia didn't look at him, but she could feel his eyes on her.

Isaac shifted in his seat, turning his focus on Millie. "What is this, Mom? I told you to leave Olivia alone."

Millie reached for his hand, that smile still on her face. "You know I can't just stand by while you make the biggest mistake of your life."

The blood in Olivia's body ran cold. This time she did look at Isaac, finding a pained expression on his face. "I told you she doesn't want anything to do with me." He peeked at her then back to his mother.

"But you said if—"

"It doesn't matter what I said. Everything is working out the way it was meant to."

Millie shook her head. "I don't believe that for a second. What am I supposed to tell my friends?"

He dragged his hand down his face and let out a sigh. "You need to stop this. All of you. I know you think you're helping, but you're just not. You and your little matchmaking crew need to mind your own business. Olivia made her choice, and so did Dad—"

"Don't you say another word."

Olivia jumped and stared at Millie. This had got to be the strangest conversation she had ever experienced in her life. The tone of Millie's voice was exactly what she would have imagined she'd used when Isaac was a young boy and tracked dirt in the house.

Her tone affected Isaac in a similar way. He snapped his mouth shut and stared at her with wide eyes. He probably hadn't been spoken to like that since he was a kid.

Millie glanced from Olivia to Isaac. "For the last two weeks this woman has been miserable."

"What?" Olivia shot a look in Isaac's direction, shaking her head and holding up her hands. "I'm fine."

"Don't lie to him. You're not fine. You never smile. You're practically the definition of the color gray." Millie gestured vaguely at her. "Ever since she got back, she hasn't had the light she used to. What did you do to her?"

"Me? I didn't do anything," Isaac insisted. "She left."

Olivia straightened. "I didn't just leave. I told you that I wasn't okay with you lying to Mr. Frederickson. All I asked was that you tell him the truth. Apparently, these days people aren't required to step up anymore." She pushed away from the table and stood. Her chair toppled behind her and she gave Millie an apologetic look as she righted it. "I'm sorry. I have to get back to work."

Without another word, she rushed toward her desk. There was only one problem. She couldn't be in the same room as Isaac and not want to run back to him and tell him she wanted to work things out.

All of the memories of their time together in New York

came flooding back and washed over her like a tsunami. Isaac was the kind of guy any girl would kill for. He was smart, sweet, handsome, and wealthy to boot. The lie he'd told was solely to help Maple Gardens become something greater.

Was she being unreasonable?

Olivia peered over to where Millie and Isaac still spoke at the table and her heart crumbled just a little more. As much as she wanted to bend the rules she had in her head, she couldn't. He never admitted he was wrong. A lie was still a lie no matter how it was packaged.

Chapter Twenty-Five

Isaac glowered at his mother. "Was that really necessary?"

She shrugged. "The last time we spoke, you kept going on and on about her. I thought for sure something had blossomed between you."

"Mom, please don't say 'blossomed,'" he groaned as he twisted just enough to see if Olivia was close enough to hear. He spun toward his mother and lowered his voice. "You heard her. She doesn't want anything to do with me. So just drop it."

"I didn't hear any such thing. She said she wanted you to confess the truth to that investor of yours and you didn't."

He rolled his eyes. "I told you. He found out anyway and he didn't seem to mind as much as I thought he would. Everything is settled between me and him."

"Then what's the problem?"

"Nothing is the problem. I got the business deal. Maple Gardens is going to start opening in different parts of the country and I can go back to doing what I do best."

Millie scowled at him and he stilled.

"*What?*"

"What are you going to do about Olivia?"

Isaac let out another groan. "I'm going to leave her alone like she wanted."

"That's it? You two spend a wonderful week together and break up over one miscommunication?"

"That's what people do, Mom. People leave."

She leveled him with another one of her glares. "You don't believe that."

"It's what Dad did."

Millie threw her hands into the air. "For heaven's sake, Isaac. Olivia is not your father. She's a wonderful girl who wasn't making any unreasonable requests. You should apologize."

"Apologize for what? She knew what we were doing going into this. She signed the contract. I could sue her for . . ." His voice died in his throat as he got another one of those looks. His shoulders dropped and he let loose a heavy breath. "Even if I tried to make things right, there is no guarantee she would accept it. You saw how mad she was."

His mother leaned over and patted his cheek. "True love always finds a way." She got to her feet and walked around him.

Isaac spun around, his eyes following her. "Where are you going?"

"I'm going to play bingo. I suggest you come up with a game plan. With a little bit of luck, you'll have her back in your arms by Christmas Eve." He got to his feet to follow her but she spun around, stopping him. "What do you think you're doing?"

"I'm playing bingo. That's what you wanted me to come for today, isn't it?"

The sly smile that touched her lips proved otherwise.

"You came for exactly what I wanted you to come for. Go on. Figure out what you can do to make this right."

"What am I supposed to do? You can't make someone love you."

"From what I can tell, that's not your problem."

Isaac opened his mouth then shut it. He glanced to where Olivia usually sat but she wasn't there.

Millie laughed. "Just think about how you can set things right and I'm sure you'll come up with the right thing. I'll see you Christmas Eve." She wandered toward the bingo room, leaving him trying to piece together what she'd said. It couldn't be that easy.

His eyes flitted to Olivia's empty desk.

Or could it?

He pulled out his phone and strode toward the exit. The second Bart picked up, he barked, "I'm going to need your help."

"I know it's tradition, Izzie, but I really don't feel like going out tonight." Olivia dropped like a heap of potatoes onto her bed and stared at the ceiling with the phone glued to her ear.

"But we always—"

"You have a fiancé now. Go out with him."

"*Olivia*," Izzie admonished. Olivia could vividly see her friend's disapproving face floating in her mind. "You need to get out. It's Christmas Eve. We can go do karaoke or we can get a drink. You need to do something. You can't just sit at home all night. Besides, when have I ever asked you for anything?"

She turned over on her side. Normally she would have

been the one dragging Izzie out to do something fun. Now the roles had flipped. Closing her eyes, she knew she'd regret it, but Izzie was right. "Fine. *One* drink. Then I'm back here and you're out doing whatever it is you and Bart want to make your own tradition."

"Deal. We're right outside."

"We? Izzie, I thought this was just going to be—"

Izzie hung up before Olivia could finish her argument.

Dang it.

The closest pair of shoes were the boots Isaac had bought her for their trip. They happened to be the only Christmassy thing she owned at the moment. She would have loved to put on her red slippers just to make Izzie mad, but she could only find one of them.

With a huff, she yanked her boots onto her feet and hurried down to the waiting car. Bart sat in the driver's seat and offered her a smile. "Glad you could make it."

"Yeah," Olivia muttered. "This is gonna be so much fun."

Bart glanced at her again. "I hope you don't mind, but we have a few presents we need to drop off at Maple Gardens for Margaret and Uncle Lawrence."

"Seeing as I'm practically a hostage, I don't see why not." Olivia leaned back and gazed out the window. It was a colder night than usual, but the sky was clear and the stars shone bright enough to put Christmas lights to shame.

Bart and Izzie held hands over the console that separated them and talked quietly in the front. They made the perfect couple. But even their relationship hadn't been without its problems. If they could get past those hurdles, then maybe she had a chance to get past hers. Christmas music played on the radio and her thoughts drifted to Isaac.

The more time she spent thinking about him, the more she knew she still wanted to be with him. She'd fallen for him—hard. She thought she could come home and just get back into the normal swing of things, but who was she kidding?

Isaac still consumed her thoughts and she didn't want anyone else.

They pulled up in front of the building and Olivia remained in her seat. Izzie got out, then leaned in to ask, "You coming?"

"No. I think I'll just stay here."

Her friend pouted. "My mom would love to see you."

"She literally sees me every day," Olivia offered, though a smile tugged at her lips.

"Please?"

Olivia sighed. "Fine. One quick visit then we get our drink and then you take me home." She shook her head and climbed out. But Olivia and Bart were already halfway around the side of the building. Why were they heading to the back?

She slammed the door shut and hurried after them. "Guys!" she called. "If you want me to come with, don't just leave me here . . ." Her feet refused to move as she rounded the side of the building. She'd somehow crossed into a different dimension.

Before her was a winter wonderland complete with snow and a "north pole." Standing in the center of tiny Christmas village houses was the one person she couldn't make herself forget.

Isaac was dressed in a suit. He wore a red scarf and in his hand he held something red. Dangling Christmas lights were strung up on candy-cane striped poles, bringing the whole scene together. All that was missing was an ice-skating rink—and she wouldn't have put it past him to figure out a way to make that happen.

Her mouth fell open as her gaze swept over the scene before landing on him. She trudged through the homemade snow along the sidewalk to where he stood. "Isaac? What are you—" Her eyes dipped to the item in his hand. "Is that my slipper?"

Isaac held it up and fidgeted with it. "Yeah."

"What are you doing with it?"

His gaze locked onto hers. "I'm sorry."

Olivia blinked then looked at the slipper again. "For taking my slipper?"

He chuckled.

Boy, she hadn't realized just how much she missed the sound of his laugh. A smile tugged at her lips but then disappeared. "What is all of this?"

Isaac took a step forward and took her hand in his. "I'm not good at this sort of thing. I realize that now."

Her heart leaped into her throat. Everything inside her shifted into overdrive as she held her breath, waiting for what he might say next.

He shook his head, his thumb running over the back of her hand. "I knew I was in love with you and yet I still messed it all up because I couldn't see past my need to expand Maple Gardens. I should have known better than to let you go. I should have fought for you. So here I am. Standing in front of this girl . . ." Isaac shifted even closer. "I guess what I'm trying to say is . . ."

"Just say it!"

They both jumped and Olivia turned to find a small audience that included about a dozen residents standing with Izzie and Bart. She let out a laugh, then covered her mouth as she turned her eyes to Isaac once more.

"I want you to know that I did try to tell Mr. Frederickson the truth after you left. He'd worked it out and you were right—the deal is still on. But that doesn't matter. It isn't Christmas without you, Olivia. I don't want to spend this one or any other without you. I'm going to spend every single day of my life proving to you that I love you. No more lies. I can't promise I'll be perfect but—"

She flung her arms around his neck and pressed her lips to his. That was all she ever wanted to hear him say. At times it had seemed so silly, but based on how happy his words had made her—at how relieved she was to hear them—she knew this was what she needed.

His arms came around her and she could vaguely hear a cheer from those watching. Her body melted against his, fitting better than any glove could. Everything she'd thought she wanted had changed into something new.

And Isaac was part of that picture now.

He deepened their kiss, pulling her feet off the snowy ground and spinning her around. A loud whirring sound kicked on; she gasped and pulled back in time to see the first bits of snow fall to the ground around them.

Isaac gave her a crooked grin. "I believe I recall that you wanted to sing carols in the snow?"

Olivia tossed her head back and laughed. "Only if I get to sing them with you."

Epilogue

Valentine's Day

Olivia leaned into Isaac as they sat in their little Sunday circle. Millie and her friends had started this little group to keep up on their children's lives, but she knew better. Her gaze swept through the small group with interest.

Who was going to be next?

She laced her fingers with Isaac's and he glanced down at her with that adoring look that still set her heart racing. He brought her hand to his lips and kissed her fingers.

Millie caught sight of the gesture and gave Olivia a warm smile before turning back to Alice's daughter. "Quinne, tell Isaac what you do for your job. I know you've told me before, but I can't remember."

Quinne glanced up from her phone. The expression on her face could only be described as boredom. She looked from Millie to Isaac and sighed. "I'm an influencer."

Isaac cocked his head to the side. "Is that a career? Do influencers actually make anything?"

Quinne raised two perfect eyebrows. "I probably make more than you."

He laughed but then that laughter died in his throat when no one else joined in. Isaac leaned forward. "You're serious?"

She nodded. "I have sponsors and events I go to. I have four-hundred million followers who listen to every word I say and then my sponsors pay me for every video I post."

Alice patted her daughter's knee. "Tell him the kind of stuff you post." She turned to the group. "It's really fascinating. She reviews products and video games."

Olivia nudged Isaac in the ribs. "That sounds better than your job. I'd love to get paid to play video games."

Isaac shot her an almost irritated look and she snickered.

"Do you have children?"

Quinne glanced at Olivia. "I don't."

"Really? That's interesting. How did you get into something like that?"

Quinne shrugged. "I guess I was in the right place at the right time." She glanced at her phone then turned to her mother. "I have to get going. I'll see you next week, okay?"

Alice nodded and reached up to give her daughter a hug. "Love you, dear."

The second Quinne was out of earshot, Alice scooted to the edge of her seat and her smile widened. "I've finally figured out who we can set her up with."

Millie and Lily's faces lit up but Isaac jumped forward before they could say a word. "No."

Olivia watched all of this with rapt interest. Her eyes bounced from person to person until they landed on Isaac.

"No more meddling. No more matchmaking."

His mother laughed. "Oh hush. If we hadn't stepped in,

then you wouldn't have Olivia. Be grateful and let us old women have what little fun we can." She turned to Alice. "Who?"

"The new chef."

Isaac groaned. He got to his feet and held out his hand to Olivia. "Come on. There's no stopping them when they get an idea in their heads."

Olivia stared at the women, disappointment seeping into her bones. "But—"

"Don't we have Valentine's Day gifts to exchange?"

Her eyes brightened and she got to her feet. "Oh yeah." She jerked her chin toward the central station. "I have yours in my desk." She tugged his hand, practically dragging him over to it, then she pulled open the drawer and grabbed the gift bag.

Isaac took the offering and removed the tissue paper. He let out a laugh as he met her gaze. "You're not serious."

"Oh, I'm deadly serious." She peered into the bag. "And I want you to try them on."

He shook his head. "I'm not wearing red fuzzy slippers in a place like this."

She pursed her lips and he laughed again, pulling her in for a lingering kiss. "They're perfect. Thank you." Then Isaac dug into his pocket and retrieved a small box. It looked too big to be a piece of jewelry . . .

Her fingers traced over the box with curiosity. "What is it?"

Isaac grinned. "Just open it."

She pried the box open and found a small couple in ice-skates embracing. They looked familiar. Olivia peered at them for a moment until she remembered where she'd seen something like this before. Her eyes widened. "These belong in the Christmas village."

He kissed the tip of her nose. "They do. And you will get a piece of your own village for every Valentine's Day, St. Patrick's Day, Birthday, Thanksgiving, Christmas, and just because . . . until your village is complete."

She held up the couple and laughed. "Do you realize how long that's going to take? There's no way I can collect them all."

"Olivia? Did you see what is under the figures? May I?"

Before she could react, Isaac gently moved the figures and lifted out another box. A small box. And then he dropped to one knee.

She gasped as he opened it, revealing an engagement ring glittering with diamonds. Time stood still and her heart with it.

"Olivia Todd, it seems we keep running into each other and although it took a while for me to get the message, I did. My life is no longer my own because you have the best part of me." Isaac's eyes shone. "You *are* the best part of me. Will you marry me?"

Tears flooded her eyes. She'd never expected to find someone to love let alone love her back. And this someone was her perfect match.

"Say yes!" Millie called and other voices chimed in with their agreement.

"Yes, Isaac. Yes, I will marry you."

And then she was in his arms and he held her tightly against his chest.

"Those pieces of the village? We might not collect them all but we have the rest of our lives to try," Isaac said.

Olivia lifted herself up to brush his lips with a soft, "A long and happy life. I love you."

PHILLIPA NEFRI CLARK

There are four books available in the Maple Gardens
Matchmaker series. More information on Phillipa's website
www.phillipaclark.com

About the Author

Phillipa lives just outside a beautiful town in country Victoria, Australia. She also lives in the many worlds of her imagination and stockpiles stories beside her laptop.

She writes from the heart about love, dreams, secrets, discovery, the sea, the world as she knows it... or wishes it could be. She loves happy endings, heart-pounding suspense, and characters who stay with you long after the final page.

With a passion for music, the ocean, animals, nature, reading, and writing, she is often found in the vegetable garden pondering a new story.

Free short book when you join Phillipa's monthly newsletter (book chat, pets, gardens, puzzles, first-looks and competitions).

www.phillipaclark.com

Also by Phillipa Nefri Clark

Detective Liz Moorland

Lest We Forgive

Lest Bridges Burn

Lest Tides Turn

Connected to this series through several characters is

Last Known Contact

Rivers End Romantic Women's Fiction

The Stationmaster's Cottage

Jasmine Sea

The Secrets of Palmerston House

The Christmas Key

Taming the Wind

Temple River Romantic Women's Fiction

The Cottage at Whisper Lake

The Bookstore at Rivers End

The House at Angel's Beach

Charlotte Dean Mysteries

Christmas Crime in Kingfisher Falls

Book Club Murder in Kingfisher Falls

Cold Case Murder in Kingfisher Falls

Plan to Murder in Kingfisher Falls

Festive Felony in Kingfisher Falls

Daphne Jones Mysteries

Daph on the Beach

Time of Daph

Till Daph Do Us Part

The Shadow of Daph

Tales of Life and Daph

Bindarra Creek Rural Fiction

A Perfect Danger

Tangled by Tinsel

Maple Gardens Matchmakers

The Heart Match

The Christmas Match

The Menu Match

The Cookie Match

Doctor Grok's Peculiar Shop Short Story Collection

Simple Words for Troubled Times

(Short non-fiction happiness and comfort book)